13 Years Later

Officer Jones

There was a 911 call in my area, so I took it even though I was just getting off work. It was 8:00 am in the morning, and I just got done working a double shift. I was told that all officers on duty were to stop what they were doing and head over there. The person was armed and dangerous. The directions were to proceed with caution. I knew that place very well; it was up to me to handle the problem.

There were bodies everywhere throughout the hallway of the building. There were people pulling at me as they took their last breath asking for help. I told them to hold on and that help was on its way. I pulled out my weapon as I searched through the building without backup. I couldn't wait for anyone else because someone's life

1

could be taken at this very moment. I never thought I would

be back here at this place, but I was hoping that I wouldn't

have to take matters into my own hands.

There he was lying on the floor covered in blood

with a blunt object in his hand. I told him to drop the

weapon and to lay face down on the floor. He laid there

silently with the weapon in hand facing the other direction.

I continue to yell, but he didn't pay any attention to me.

What was he thinking? I knew that at any moment that my

backup would come and I wouldn't be able to save him.

Michael

There was a bright white light surrounding me, and I can't move. I can hear voices in the background. I don't know where I am, and I can't see a thing. What is going on? Is this the end? As I started questioning my own existence my life started to flash before my eyes. Everything that I went through was coming full circle, and all I could do is watch it play out.

I was born and raised in Chicago, but I had to move with my Aunt to Casperton, Louisiana at a very young age. My aunt arrived one day after school. I was taken away from everything I had ever known on my 13th birthday. Now 13 years later I am fighting for my life. I can still taste the frosting from my birthday cake that my Mom made just for my special day. There were balloons and decorations all over the house. I can remember sitting at the kitchen table when my aunt took me away and then later that day my aunt coming to get me. I didn't have the chance to say goodbye to anyone. Everything happened so quickly without any explanation. The only thing my aunt told me was that I needed to go with her right away. I couldn't talk to anyone, get close to anyone, or tell them anything about my past.

I have one older sister, a niece and a Mom. My Dad and I were very close and I could tell him anything. I can remember my Dad teaching me how to ride a bike, play basketball and how to fight off bullies. My Mom and I were close as well, but not as close as I was to my Dad. I was his only son, so I will always carry on his legacy by being a junior.

A couple of months went by, and I didn't even get a phone call from my family. I asked my aunt why hasn't anyone called me, and she told me that it was complicated. I started to get this really bad headache, and from then on it started to happen frequently. I missed my family, and friends. I want to go home. I don't know anyone here, and I don't understand what is going on. My father and I didn't talk after I moved, and when I came home to visit nothing was ever the same.

I had only been in town for a few months, and out of nowhere Andrew Earnest Smith III appeared. He was a small, timid, gullible, naïve and quiet guy. Even though we had nothing in common we still manage to become great friends. We did everything together. I made sure that no one messed with him as long as I was around. I kind of felt sorry for the little guy. His family wasn't your typical family and his father was very strict.

He told me about his weekend visit back to Chicago, and how he didn't want to go back. I didn't know that we both were Chicagoans. So, I guess we did have more in common than I thought. But his weekend visits seemed as though they were pulled right out of a horror movie.

My little buddy talked to himself a lot, and had a very active imagination. He had a special place he went to when he wanted to escape from all the problems in his life. He told me that in this place he was able to control the outcome. "I am the champion and the best fighter in the whole universe in my special place," Andrew yelled out! No matter what he was going through to me he was my little buddy. I didn't see a kid with problems, but an individual who was simply unique. We all are unique individuals and different in our own special way.

I wished he could have spent time with me and my family. His family kept a close eye on him. He was heavily guarded, and even I had a hard time hanging out with him. The kid had problems that I couldn't even imagine on my worst day. I felt sorry for him, and tried to be there for him.

Since we were best buds we found ways to hangout and no one ever caught on. I never went to his special place, but I knew back then he needed a safe place of his own. I didn't understand until now why he didn't want my help. He wanted to fight his own battles even if it took the rest of his life doing so.

He spent two months during the summer with his family in Chicago while I spent two weeks there with my Aunt Katherine. Auntie Katherine is my Dad's sister. She is a self – made millionaire. She owns boutiques and her own clothing line all across America, and has been talking my ear off about going international. I enjoyed my two weeks, but I could only do so much to protect him before I had to go back. When I went back home my aunt was always there with me when I spent time with my family. She told me that in time she would tell me the truth, but until then I had to trust her. We all had fun together, so her being there made it extra special.

Andrew and Mr. Smith didn't get along at all. Mr. Smith worked at night and after work he would come home drunk. He didn't like it when his Dad would come home drunk. His father use to come into his bedroom and tell him it was time to play. The games Mr. Smith and Andrew played at night weren't fun at all. Mr. Smith told him all the time that is how a father and son play together. He was told that if he ever spoke a word of this to anyone that they would take him away to another family that would be mean to him.

So ever night like clockwork Mr. Smith came into his son's room and played their father and son game with him. Mrs. Smith and their daughter, Tiffany didn't say a word and ignored the screams that came out of the room every night. I told Andrew if he wanted I would take care of the situation. I would have made sure that Mr. Smith never played those father and son games with him ever again. He didn't want to cause any problems, and thought if I did something that it would just make matters worse.

I didn't know how much longer I could stand by, and let my best friend go through this. Mr. Smith will pay for this, but until then I will respect his decision. But when

the time comes I promise Mr. Smith will pay for everything
he has done. He has picked on the wrong person's friend,
and I am not like Andrew I will fight back.

My life wasn't like Andrews, but I did have my
own struggles. I guess everyone goes through their own
trials and tribulations. When I looked at his life compared
to mine I guess my life isn't so bad after all. No one can
walk in someone else's shoes and expect to get the same
outcome. What I am going through is the journey that I
have to take on my own and no one else. Unlike him I am
ready for whatever life has in store for me.

Have I lived a full and rewarding life? I can't tell
you that, but what I can tell you is that it wasn't boring. We
tend to think just because things don't seem exciting, then
we are lacking substance in our lives. No one can bring
meaning to your life, so you have to have an open mind.
You have to be willing to challenge yourself, and be open
to doing new things. No matter what I did in my life; I

always tried to live with no regrets. In the end what you get out of life is what you make of it. I was so blinded by what I didn't have that I couldn't appreciate what I did have.

Looking back on my life as a child I couldn't help but wonder what ever happened to my best friend Andrew. I made a promise to him and I regret to this very day that I didn't keep that promise. Without me around to protect Andrew I wonder what would become of him. Forces beyond my control kept him and me away from one another.

Andrew was the kid that everyone picked on and no one respected. No one wanted to play with him or become his friend besides me. I thought of him as an individual that just marched to a different beat than everyone else. I saw the real Andrew that nobody else saw. I knew that deep down inside of him there was a person that everyone else would enjoy seeing. When I was around everyone got a chance to see how fun, exciting and brave he was. Too bad I couldn't have been there for Andrew when he needed me the most, but sometimes things are beyond a person's control.

Growing up I was always the brave, tough, smart and the most athletic kid on the block. Everyone respected me and wanted to be my friend. Even though I always had friends part of me always felt alone. I guess in that respect I could relate to Andrew and that is probably why we grew so close. The bond that we shared was unbreakable. When I had to leave town I thought about him all the time. I knew that the two of us would always be connected to one another no matter what.

I felt Andrew's pain and suffering. My life and my problems paled in comparison to what he had to go through. I hope Mr. Smith paid for what he did to Andrew because if I ever get my hands on him he would regret everything he has ever done to Andrew. God have mercy on Mr. Smith's soul because when I see him I will not show any mercy.

My family isn't perfect, but growing up I felt that something just wasn't right. I had everything I could ever ask for. For some odd reason I couldn't help but feel something lacking in my life and wanted answers. Part of me felt that my life was incomplete and that I needed the final piece of the puzzle in place to move on with my life. I had questions and I wanted answers.

I guess you can say I am an optimist and I believe that everything happens for a reason. There is a higher power at work and I am here to serve him. My purpose in life is to go on the path set out for me and to follow it until I end up in heaven. For some reason my path has been broken and I am lost. I don't know what direction to turn in or if I am currently walking on the wrong path. Life was so much easier when I was a child. I guess I was too busy watching out for my little buddy that I didn't realize I had my own life to live.

I can remember my first job. Andrew and I were only 17 years old when we got a job at Whacky Warehouse on Mills Road in Casperton. Andrew and I never worked together, but everyone liked him there. He was a good worker, and always was willing to lend a helping hand. I can remember the day I left because that was the day that my little buddy life changed forever.

Andrew was a good kid, but he didn't know how to handle the world as I did. Most people would find ways to adjust and overcome obstacles. Andrew on the other hand had a hard time being himself. I had to be my little buddies eyes and ears. I didn't want the world to eat him alive. Besides, Andrew promised to save me if the world was taken over by the zombies, which always left me with a smile on my face.

There was this young woman named Stacy who Andrew had a crush on. Stacy was a 21 year old reception at the warehouse that we worked at. Andrew would come in early just to see her, and help her before he started. Everyone in the company knew that Stacy was a nice person, and would never want to hurt Andrew's feelings. He used to come in every week with a gift for Stacy. At first everyone thought it was cute, but when he started to say she was his girlfriend it started to get a little creepy. I tried to talk to Andrew, but he didn't want to listen. He believed that Stacy wanted to be with him, but didn't want anyone else to know. She told him on several occasions that he was her work boyfriend. But I think he took the playful jester a little bit too far.

I knew that someday this was going to cause a serious problem. So, one day Andrew saw Stacy flirting with Donald who was a stock room crew worker. Stacy was the receptionist, so there would be guys from the stock room coming to visit her from time to time. He saw Donald reach over and touch Stacy's hand. Stacy wore a necklace with a heart charm on it, and Andrew use to daydream about her putting it around his neck all the time. When Andrew saw him talking to her it pushed him over the edge.

I was sleeping, and then later that night I checked my voicemail. I had 15 missed calls and voicemails. Andrew had called me crying about Donald trying to steal his girlfriend away from him. He said, "She is my girl.....She is my girlfriend....So hands off Donald....Hands off my girlfriend!"

I told him to calm down, and to not do anything foolish. I knew that if he went into work with the same mindset that he would get himself in a lot of trouble. Donald was a bit of a tough guy, and didn't back down from anyone. If Andrew went into work the next day trying to push him around, then he would be asking for a death wish.

I told Andrew to get some sleep, and that I would personally handle the situation myself tomorrow. All I wanted to do was talk to Donald. I was going to tell him if you see Andrew coming just make sure not to do anything with Stacy around him.

However, what happened the next day at work was far from what I expected. I calmly walked up to Donald, and told him to be try to understand what is going on with Andrew, and to respect his feeling. But Donald being a jerk pushed me, and told me to take off. So, I did what I would have normally done if someone challenged my manhood. I had beaten him within an inch of his life. There was blood all over me. I never saw so much blood before, and he laid their covered in his own blood.

I went to the restroom to clean myself up. I didn't have any guilt of remorse for what I did. I kept the blood stain on my clothes, and wore it like a badge of honor. After I washed my face I looked up, and there was Andrew staring at me in the mirror. He looked at me with a terrified look on his face.

Pacing back and forth he says, "You messed everything up Michael! I had everything under control. Now we're in big trouble Mike. We're in big trouble. I will handle it Mike, so don't you worry I will save the day. Don't you worry about a thing Mike! I will defeat the dragon, and save the princess."

Don't do anything Andrew. You have done enough already little buddy. I handled the problem. They will not be bothering us again. So, don't you worry about a thing Andrew I will handle it. Go home get some rest, and by this time tomorrow everything will be fine. I will make sure nothing happens to either of us. But you have to promise me that no matter what you will never let anyone hurt you again. I may not always be here, so promise me that you will never let anyone hurt you again.

Andrew pulled out his imaginary sword, and says, "I promise you Mike that I will never let anyone hurt me again. I promise you that I will protect you and everyone I love. Together you and I will conquer the world maybe even the universe. No one can stop us Mike! We make a great team Mike!"

I have to go Andrew, so you take care of yourself. Don't ~~get~~ forget what I asked of you little buddy. Never let anyone change who you are. Always be yourself, and don't let them take away your special place. Maybe someday I can find my own special place. Until we meet again little buddy take care of yourself.

Andrew waved goodbye, and says, "I will see you tomorrow Mike."

Stacy got a little drunk that night, and started posting pictures of her drinking at the club with Donald. She also posted comments on her social media sight. She was saying that she had a little secret that she wanted to share with the world. So, I paid Stacy a little visit the next

day. Of course she was with Donald at work hung-over.

Donald told me to leave, and that he would expose the

company's dirty little secret. Stacy laughed and smiled, ~~and~~ She

says, "Watch the video on my phone, and tell me if this

isn't worth giving us a million dollars. Donald and I are

going to be rich! Don't you worry we will give you

something for keeping your mouth shut until we get what

we want."

Give me all the footage and delete it from your

phone. I promise you both that I will forget this ever

happened. If you don't give me what I want, it will not be

good for either of you. Do ~~both~~ you understand what I am

saying?

Donald gets in my face, and says, "You got lucky

last time, but I don't think you will have the same outcome.

So if you want to leave in one piece I suggest you go now.

Don't think because you ~~was~~ are teacher's pet that you can do whatever you want around here. Things are different now, and the rules have changed. Stacy and I are in control of what happens from here on out."

I started to get a headache again, and this time it started to rip through my brain like it was being cut with a knife. I think I blacked out because when I woke up I was at Andrew's house. Andrew says, "I saw you talking to them, but I stayed hidden like a ninja. I didn't say a word, and I kept quiet just like you said. I let you handled it. I closed my eyes, and when I opened them they were gone. You were laying there on the ground, so I called Mr. Stevenson to come take you back to my house. He said ok little buddy, and helped us out. I told him that we fixed the problem, but he was upset. He told me that he was going to handle it, and then he went home."

I thought that she was a nice person, and was trying to help. I guess I was wrong, and they both were out for a big paid day. She had recorded Donald having sex with our boss Mr. Stevenson, and a minor in a hotel room. She vowed to take it to the local newspapers if I got in trouble for what I did to him. I now know that was a lie, and they were planning to leak the video even after Mr. Stevenson paid them.

So my aunt told me to leave town, and that it wasn't safe there anymore. She told me that she would pay for a one way ticket to Paris. My aunt promised me money to live off of, a car, and any house waiting for me in Paris. But I couldn't take her money or anything from her. She was good to me, and I didn't want to take advantage of her. I wanted to go back home, and be with my family. I haven't heard from them in a while.

My aunt told me not to go home, and it wasn't safe in Chicago anymore. I couldn't get in contact with my family, so I used the money that I saved up to go back to Chicago. I didn't tell anyone where I was going. After that day I left town, and Andrew behind. Andrew kept calling me, but I didn't answer. I couldn't help him this time, he was on his own. I didn't see, or talked to him after that day.

I was sorry for leaving my little buddy, but I had to move on with my life. Nothing was going right, so I had to make the necessary changes to better my situations. I had to look within myself, and find out who I wanted to become before the man that I didn't want to be became who I am. But like the leaves that filled the trees of life, this feeling I had only lasted for a season.

When I arrived home it felt cold and dark. My Mom, sister and niece were sitting there at the table not paying any attention to me. My Dad wasn't there, and it seem as though he had been gone for a while. There were no clothes, but pictures on the wall of him. The pictures we took were when we all were one big happy family.

No one noticed I was home, and no one seemed to care. I felt as though I was all alone in a crowded room. I waved to get someone attention, but everyone went about their days as if I wasn't there. As the days went on no one left the house, or made an effort to do anything. I felt like a ghost in my own home.

My aunt kept calling me, but I didn't answer her calls. There was a police car that drove passed the house every day, and stopped for a minute before it drove away. I was the only one who left the house to go to work. After a while I felt that my family all changed for the worst when my Dad died. No on hasn't been the same since he passed away. He passed away around the time I had to move, but after that I didn't come back to visit. I guess my family felt as though I disserted them.

It has been ten years or so and I haven't seen my Aunt Katherine. After a few years the calls stopped. I eventually changed my number, but she still felt like she was close by. I didn't want to call, but I wanted answers about my Dad. She told me that he was in a car accident by a hit and run driver. The guy who hit my Dad was never found. My Dad was rushed to the hospital and died later that night in the emergency room. She wanted me to come back home, but I said no. I hung up, and that was the last time that I talked to my Aunt.

My Mom hasn't talked to me about his death. I didn't go to the funeral, and I don't even know entire story behind his death. Everyone is acting weird around me. No one talks to me, or barely looks at me. It is like I am on the outside looking in. Everyone keeps to themselves. It is like I am not even here, or I am in a living nightmare.

Day after day I worked at the Steel Mill Company, and nothing has changed. My family still acts as though I don't exist. Everyone seems to be in their own little world, and I am on the outside looking in. I felt all alone, and didn't know what to do. Should I call my aunt? I can't call aunt Katherine now after all these years has gone by. What would I say to my aunt especially after going against her rules?

I am thirty years old now and the years are going by so fast. I feel like I haven't accomplished half of the things that I wanted to. Nothing in my life seems to be going right and I am working at a dead end job. As I watched my former classmates all go on to great careers I feel like I am taking a back seat to everyone. Everyone else has all the answers to their questions as I am still pondering what direction I am heading in.

What is it about the unknown that intrigues us and keeps us wanting to know more? I don't know if I believe that curiosity killed the cat, but I do believe that we should all be aware that we aren't meant to know everything. Sometimes I look up into the sky and wonder what heaven is like. Is heaven as great as everyone thinks it is? I see churches everywhere, which makes me wonder if God is watching over them all.

Does the devil really exist or is he just a myth that puts a face to evil? I am not sure if there is life after death, aliens on other planets, or when we die we go to a better place. There is only one thing that I can be absolute certain about is the power that comes from faith. If you believe in something with your heart and soul then whether it's true or not is irrelevant.

Truth is only as real as you make of it and believing in something doesn't have to be proven because what you believe in your heart is what matters the most. I use to think that God had set a special path for me that would instantly propel me into a successful career.

When I graduated college I thought that I would find a job right away and then I would be able to buy my mother a mansion. I could ask my Aunt Katherine for money, a job, or a big house, but I felt that I had to earn it my way. I thought that I would land a great job so my mother wouldn't have to work again, and a job where I could be proud of. Everyone at my job was wishing me luck, and saying that within a month I would be gone on to bigger and better things.

I went to Dent University of Chicago. I graduated with honors, and I thought the sky was the limit for me. I was working a full time job, and going to school. When I finally graduated I felt that all my hard work was about to pay off. The sleepless nights, the cramming for test, and countless hours I put in had to amount to something. Everything had to work out in the end that is how it supposes to go for a struggling college student when they reach the finish line.

However, I have been at my job 5 years, which was longer than I expected with no other job opportunities in sight. Working at the local Steel Mill isn't a bad job, but it's just not for me. This wasn't the life I had envisioned for myself. I feel like I am stuck here, and I have no way out. Should I settle, and take it for what it is? Maybe it is too late for me to reach for my goals and dream.

My coworkers made my job worth going to especially April. I had a crush on her, and she knew it. She was dating my other coworker Jonathan. They were very happy together, but I could see her looking in my direction from time to time. I didn't want to complicate things, or ruin her life. All I wanted was an opportunity to show her that I was a better man, and that I could make her happy. She deserved the best, and I don't think he was giving her all that she deserved.

I remember the first time I made my move; it was a few years later at the annual Christmas party. She was wearing a black dress, a tinker bell bracelet and her hair was blowing in the wind like she was an angel. I asked her to dance, and she said yes. All eyes were on us, but it felt as though we were the only two in the room. It seemed as though the song lasted for an eternity. After the song was over Jonathan grabbed April's hand, and said it was time to go.

April looked back at me, and waved good-bye. I knew that she wanted me, but didn't want to break her boyfriend's heart. It was only a matter of time before she would come to me, and say that I was the one that she wanted all along. It was only a matter of time before she realized who the real man was. All I had to do was sit back and wait.

I went to the restroom, and to my surprise Andrew was there. I couldn't believe he had followed me back to Chicago. I looked at him and he looked at me. I told him that he had to go, but then April came in. Andrew started talking and for some reason April was smitten with Andrew. She took Andrew's hand and left the restroom. All I could do is watch the love of my life leave with my little buddy Andrew. How could he betray me?

I stayed close, and kept my mouth closed. I had to find out what was going on, and what was about to happen. Was Andrew's first time going to be with the love of my life? April took Andrew to her car. I could see her kissing him. She was on top of him, and I could see Andrew face, and he was terrified. He didn't know what to do, or how to react. I couldn't help my little buddy. This time my little buddy was on his own, and about to make a journey from a boy to a man in a matter of minutes. With a blink of an eye it was over. Andrew was a man, and April walked away with the heart of my buddy in the palm of her hands.

A few days passed, and I haven't spoken to April. Jonathan came into work saying that he hasn't heard, or seen April since the night of the Christmas party. April wasn't at her apartment. He stated "Her friends or family didn't know where she was." Just like that April vanished, and was never heard from again. I don't know what ever happened to April, but I always wondered what could have been. It was supposed to be April and I together. April was supposed to be my future wife, but Andrew ruined that. I knew that Jonathan wasn't any competition for me, but my little buddy turned out to be a wild card in my plans to win her heart.

After the night of my Christmas party Andrew also vanished. I didn't see my little buddy again, and he didn't even say good-bye. I don't know why he came back, and why would he leave so suddenly. Did Andrew and April disappear in the night together? All I know is that my special moment turned into Andrew's special moment. At this point I was glad that I left my little buddy behind because a friend wouldn't have stepped in the way of true love. Where ever he is now I hope he stays there.

My attitude is slowly going from compassionate to pessimistic. I am getting sick and tired of people saying that I need hands on experience. So, I will stop at nothing to become successful, but at the same time I will not let anyone stand in my way. I am constantly evolving, and as the days am becoming a more rational person. I see the world differently now and it's not perfect.

The world is very complex and America is not the land of the free as the government wants us to believe. I believe that I have to go get what I want and worry about what I need later. I can't do anything for someone else I have to think about myself first. You must first love yourself before you can love others. Survival of the fittest seems like a natural way of living and there are some that may not have a problem with living the weakness behind.

So, I am starting to pray less after things I wanted in life seemed to fall on deaf ear with God. I started to talk to my Dad who was watching me from up above. God was becoming a distant memory to me, and I was losing touch with what real happiness was about. I use to think that happiness is what you make of it no matter if you are rich or poor. I also use to believe that you must crawl before you could walk, and that your experiences in life make you stronger to overcome the next obstacle that awaits you in life.

However, I now believe that nothing is meant to be, destiny doesn't have a role in my life, and good people aren't all blessed with good fortunes. I believe that it is the survival of the fittest and I will not be weak anymore like the rest that has fallen. I must be strong, and step on a few people to get to the top.

I looked in the mirror, and told myself to snap out of it. The whining had to cease, and I had a lot of growing up to do. Complaining wasn't going to get me anywhere, so why bother. Growing up I was always confident, strong, and brave. Now I am turning into my little buddy, which isn't necessarily a bad thing.

I started to get those headaches again, and at first they weren't that bad. As time when on my headaches got worse. One minute I felt as though I could do anything, and the next minute I felt like giving up. Advil became my best friend, and eventually I started to feel a little better. Life wasn't so bad after all, but I had a bad feeling deep inside of me that this was only the beginning of what was to come.

Time was no longer important to me. Minutes, hours, and days would go by unnoticed. I went to work like I always did, but felt detached from the world. What it me, or was the way I was feeling was the realization of how pathetic my life was? I don't know what I am doing anymore, who I am, or what I am to become.

I calmed myself down and came back to my senses. So, I held my head up high and tried my best to believe that anything was possible if you believed that it was. My faith and hope is all I have to hold onto. Hopefully someday I can make a difference in the world. I have always believed I had a higher calling in life. I am a just tired of going through these trials and tribulations. There are some people that can be trusted, so I will have to try to only keep positive people around me.

My mood and attitude started to change rapidly like night and day. One minute I had an upbeat attitude and the next minute I was mad at the world. When I came home from work I would lock myself in my room thinking to myself that I am all alone in this world. I currently stay with my sister, my niece and mom. Even with my family by my side I felt like I was all alone.

Negativity stuck to me like a badge of honor. Everything I saw and did angered me. Everything that went right to me was on the path to go wrong. Pessimism was pumped through my vein and into my heart. The glass in my life was always half empty at this point and I had an opinion for anything that was going on in the world.

I was starting to get sick of people making excuses and not owning up to what they have done. No one protected my little buddy Andrew from his Dad? No one stopped my Aunt Katherine from taking me from my family as a child. Everyone wants someone to help them, but the people that really needs help gets left out in the cold. It is survival of the fittest, and only the strongest will survive in the end.

Society is so messed up; it's just getting colder and colder. That is why I choose to stop fighting because I can't fight anymore. The last battle I fought was back in Louisiana and that was to help out a friend. Now I am at this point in my life I am on the brink of giving up hope of salvation. Why should I care when the people in the world don't care if I live or die?

We live in a time where everyone thing has to have a cause and effect. Does everything happen for a reason? I don't know if everything happens for a reason, but I guess only time will tell.

Everyone wants to be different, but in the end we all die. Nothing can stop the inevitable. We can fight and fight all we want, but in the end are we in control of our lives? Everyone deserves a place in this world even it is hiding in the shadow of one's self. My buddy wanted to fit in, and just have a place in this world without judgment, ridicule, or harm. No one should ever feel like they don't have a voice, but at the same time no one should believe that their voice is the only one that should be heard.

No one wants to fight to save humanity. When I was growing up I wanted to protect my little buddy from harm, and he wanted to save the universe. I don't think people should pray to God only when things are bad, but to thank him when things are going good as well. Knowing deep down inside they only care about themselves.

I am sick and tired of trying to do right, and when everything eventually goes terribly wrong. Praying to God for help at night now is like talking to the wind. I see nothing when I talk to him, but all I feel is a breeze that's only there for a moment. So, God is you only here to give me hope for the moment, and in the end let me sit here in wallow in doubt of your existence? Because I am now starting to believe that if you are real that you don't have time to hear what I have to say.

I was beginning to feel like I had lost my sense of reality and everything around me started to change before my eyes. Everyone around me started to look, talk and act differently around me. My world was turned upside down and I was trying to hold on for dear life. Now I know how my little buddy Andrew felt and now my path in life mirrored his.

Without questions what was happening to me was new territory for me that for the first time in my life I was afraid to embark on. I watched my dreams crash and burn over my fragile desires. I felt like I was right all along about how nothing great will ever happen to me. I felt as though I have reached the end of the road of my life and I have nowhere else to go.

I had to get my focus back and give myself one more chance to become successful. No one or nothing was going to stand in my way to be truly happy. I was ready for the fight, and ready to deliver the knockout punch. It was now clear to me that what I had to do was play a little dirty and step on a few people until I got enough power to help others.

Who am I kidding? I didn't want to help anyone. Sometimes I wonder where all this rainbow and unicorn talk is coming from? This concept that I wanted to help the world wasn't me. I was there for Andrew, but that was the only person I would ever protect. My family is my family and I will always be on their side. But the rest of the world like me had to do things with no help.

So, I had to man up to everything that was going on. I had to search deep inside myself, and find out what I really wanted. Because I can sit here all day crying over what I don't have. I can complain about how much the world has wronged me, but at the end of the day it will be me wasting my breath.

I didn't quite understand why things ended up happening the way they did? No one knows what their future holds. The present time to me felt like I was on a bus, and my final destination was my future. The stops that I made along the way would eventually define who I was going to be. I wished I would have always felt that way because I didn't. Everything at this point in my life had led me to this moment. I was all for it until one day, one morning, one event in time changed my life forever.

Chapter 2

It was about 11:30 pm and my cell phone rang. A guy trying to sell me something said, "It is time for you to get the answer that you seek. Are you ready to go on your journey?" I hung up the phone thinking it was a prank call, but the guy called back. I told him that I didn't want what he was trying to sell. How did this crazy guy get my number? The salesman told me that he had an offer of a lifetime and that I would be crazy not to hear him out.

So, I was a little curious about what the man had to offer, so I listened to what he had to say. "Imagine being able to go to heaven or hell before you die, and being able to live to talk about it. Imagine being about to go to a place where good is at peace, and evil is surrounded by torture. You have an opportunity to go to a place that people can only dream about, so I ask you are you someone that wants his dreams to come true?" I thought this guy was a crazy for saying this, "So I told him that you need to seek some help and to take my name off the list."

But before I could hang up the phone; he told me that my Dad will be there waiting for me in heaven. He told me that my Dad has been watching me since the day he left, is proud of me. He also told me that my dad can't wait to have a long talk with me like we use to do when he was alive. I didn't know what to say but, "Where will my dad be?"

The guy said, "Come to Crossroad Park at midnight tomorrow, and all will be revealed." I said tell me who you are, and how do you know about my father; answer me damn it; answer me! The phone clicked and then he was gone. Can this be real, or is this guy messing with my head? How does this guy know so much about me and my dad? There is no way that he could look up information like that, or ask someone. Can someone I know be playing a cruel joke on me; or am I being made a fool of? God what is going on? I stayed up most of the night thinking about the salesmen and our conversation, and came to the conclusion that this guy is nuts.

I got up for work like I always do, and then I left the house to find an envelope next to my front door with my name on it.

It was a ticket with THE ROAD LEADING TO HEAVEN AND HELL and ROUND TRIP on it in big letters. I started to look around, and freak out. My sister came out to see what was wrong with me. I wanted to tell her, but part of me didn't want her to tell me to tear up the ticket because it's not real. That was the first time I talked to my sister in years. I didn't even think she remembered I still existed. This has been a weird day for me. First the letter and now my sister is talking to me. What else will happen to me today?

So, I told her that I think I lost my ID for work and I am going to be late. So, I put the ticket in my jacket as I pretended to look for my ID and then pulled it out like I had found it. Here it goes I told my sister. My sister said, "See what did I tell you before if you stop and take your time you will always find what you are looking for." I left the apartment and started walking to the bus stop as I thought about what my sister had just said. Has God finally answered my call, and this is his way of showing me that he is listening to me?

Could it be that I am searching for answers so bad that I am following lies disguised as the truth to fulfill a void in my life? I don't know what to do. Life is hard enough already, and now this. What are you trying to do to me God, or is this the work of the devil? The ticket did say the roads leading to heaven and hell. The salesmen never said that my father would be in heaven or hell. What does this all mean?

There is only one way to find out, so I will go tonight to find out the truth for myself. I can't sit back and live to regret not at least knowing if this was a waste of time. If this was my destiny, then who I am to question God? What is beyond the clouds, rational thinking, and is there life after death? I had to find out if my life had meaning. Am I here for a reason?

If this is real I want to see for myself, and tell my Dad face to face I never stopped missing him. I am at work, and time is slowly moving on, and on as the day winds down. My co-workers are trying to talk to me on our lunch break, but I am not there mentally. My mind is on tonight, and thinking of the countless possibilities that awaits me tonight.

Will I be taking a bus, a plane, or going through some kind of portal?

Will I go to heaven, or will I be going to hell. Well I will either be hugging my father as the wind brushed its warmth across my face, or sweating as flesh burns around me. I finally make it home from work, and its 8:30 pm.

Three in a half hours before I have to be at Crossroads Park, and I am starting to panic.

I changed my clothes because I didn't know whether this would be a formal or casual affair. I will be reuniting with my Dad so I want to look my best. If tonight will be my last night on earth, then I want it to be because I took a chance on something that I felt in my heart to be true. I hope that if someone finds me dead Lord that you will let them know that I didn't do it for myself. I had to find out the truth to the answers that everyone at one time questioned life after death. I told my sister that I was going out with a friend.

I told her that I would be back later and that she should not wait up for me. I didn't want to tell her the truth not right now because I was afraid that she would panic. My sister would have gotten worried, and called my mother.

I am loved and respect my Mom, so I didn't want my mother knowing that I was going on a crazy quest from a crazy man who called me late at night. I was invited by a man I do not know to go to see my father her deceased husband at a place that I am not certain that exist. If my Mom was in my shoes I believe that she would want to find out if this was real.

My Mom would want answers, and would stop at nothing to get them. I had to do this if not for myself, but for my family to know that my Dad has always been there for us even after death. This is something I have to do for all of us. I can't let my family down. I must go, and find out why I was chosen. If I could get answer maybe it would bring my family and I closer. Maybe this will give us back what we once had. I needed to know what was going on, and why things weren't going right for me.

Maybe people need to look deeper into their heart and soul and ask themselves why I am here. Can we live in a world without poverty and crime? Can we have gangs that organize to help better the community and aide authority in protecting our streets? Can men stop beating on the people they love and only raise their hands to praise the Lord up above? We need to value our lives like we value the weight in gold. Fighting to succeed, but not to the point that we have to sell our soul to get what we need. I wish all races could get on the same page by burying their hatred, prejudices and cultural differences. Respecting each other and fighting for the greater cause should be what the world stood for.

My values and belief is not what is at stake here, it is the understanding of what is lacking in my life. I believe in each and every one of us there is a desire to know why I am here. Even though we have dreams, goals and ambitions we also tend to want to know is that enough. Sure we can stay focused and obtain things on our own to live a better life. If I could get a little bit of help from someone up above I could have a wonder life.

I thank God for letting me get up every morning to even have the opportunity to complain about what I want to do with my life. My life, my struggles and my journey isn't about forcing someone to change their way of thinking. No matter what happens to me I will always believe it happened for a reason. Even when I take my last breath I will know that I gave my life my all. I may not be able to walk the walk, but I believe in time I will be ready to lace up my shoes to get it a try. I need to keep my focus because what I am about to do is by far the craziest thing I have ever considered doing.

Well at least thinking about how messed up the world is has distracted me from the really believing that there is a bus that will actually take me to my Dad. I don't believe it, but I will regret it for the rest of my life if I didn't at least see it for myself if this is real or a scam.

I am on the bus going to Crossroad Park and a million thoughts are swirling around in my mind like a tornado. Part of me wanted to get off the bus, and go back home. The other part of me wanted to see it through, and reunited with my Dad who I had wanted to tell him how much his family misses him. It seemed like the bus had stopped at every single stop, and I got even more anxious at it got closer to my stop. I finally arrive at Crossroad Park, and it's about 11:45 pm.

I looked around and there are about 100 people standing around at the park. I walk up to this guy named Spencer and he is also waiting for whatever is to come to take us to over destination. I asked Spencer how are we getting there, and do he actually believe in the life after death thing. Spencer said, "This is my second time on this trip, and am going to hell. My mother is a Christian, and she has repeated sent me on this trip hoping that I will change my ways. I told her that I am going to hell when I die, and I don't care about the afterlife.

Hell isn't so bad, and if you play your card right you could live a life of luxury with Satan. I know how this must sound, but when the bus comes it will take us to a place call Limbo, where another two bus will come to take some to heaven and the rest to hell." I was starting to think that he was psycho, and I was about to go on a bus of cult worshipers who was probably going to commit suicide. I was starting to head for the hills so to speak, and then a bus pulls up. People started to board the bus, but I stood in the back hesitant to get on board. I was the last one standing outside the bus, and the bus driver says, "Michael are you coming or not? I know that you must be scared, but all answers will be revealed after your journey has ended."

I said you are the guy I talked to on the phone yesterday aren't you? How do you know my name and so much about my family? Who are you? The guy looked at me, and smiled. He told me that his name is Paul, and he is a guide. He was the guide for God, but he treats everyone equally as he takes them to Limbo. So, I got on the bus, and then Paul the guide started to speak.

Paul says, "Hello everyone I am Paul I will be your guide today. I will be taking you all to Limbo where you all will either be getting on the bus to go to heaven or the bus to go to hell. On your tickets it has the place highlighted in blue for heaven and if you going to hell in red. You all will be placed in a room of two until the buses arrive, and then there will be an announcement for you all to board your get buses. Only a few hours will pass on earth, but it will feel like an eternity in heaven or hell.

You will wake up at the last place you slept and remember everything that happened. You must hold on to your ticket because if someone else happens to get your ticket, they will be able to take your place. This trip is not to decide your final destination after you pass on, but to give you a glimpse into what to expect if you don't change your ways or stay focused.

Remember nothing is what it seems and whatever happens here will help you deal with all the unanswered questions in your life. Thanks for taking part in this journey and good luck to you all." After that introduction I was speechless and didn't know what to say.

Spencer was sitting by me and asked me, and ask me why was I on this journey? I was started to feel sick to my stomach, but then I opened the envelope. I looked at my ticket, and heaven was highlighted in blue. Spencer said, "See kid you have nothing to worry about. You know of course hell is highlighted in red on mine." I asked Spencer what they do when you get into hell. Spencer said, "Well last year when I went hell was a lot like earth, but there you only survive by putting fear into your fellow man.

I was only able to watch from the bus because in hell you are not allowed for any reason to get off the bus. Everything around you and everything you see will give a visitor the answer that they seek. No one is safe in hell and you constantly have to watch out for hell beasts. Hell beasts are creatures that are monsters that hunt you down like prey.

They eat people who are weak and praying to God to take them away from their pain. If that wasn't enough you have to worry about people who will do anything and everything to get on Satan's good side. Satan loves killing, raping and destroying people's life in hell. Some people that are in hell are people who were snatched out of Limbo, or got tricked into coming there.

When you go to hell the bus drives around hell letting you see ever horrific thing you can possibly imagine within arm's reach, and then it parks by the portal to Limbo. The bus sits there, and strange things will happen. I started like I needed to be out there. I wanted to get a closer look at what was going on so I stepped off the bus. I saw some gigantic looking dog running towards me and it was up to me to reach that bus before the hell beasts got to me. I saw people screaming for help, and people with weapons trying to attack me.

Satan's has followers down there that would do whatever it takes to prevent you from returning to earth. After the first time I learned my lesson, so I stayed on the bus no matter what I saw. Other than that hell is like a roller coaster, it is only scary until the ride is over."

Wow, I am sorry to hear that Spencer. The only reason that I am going to heaven is to find out why I am the way I am. I need to know what my purpose is. I need to hear the truth from my father, and then I will be able to move on with my life. I wasn't planning on going on this journey, but now that I am here I feel that I have to see it through until the end. But I do hope that whatever you go through in hell will hopefully give you a new outlook on life.

All this trip is for me is to tell my Dad how I was feeling and maybe he can help me find my purpose. My life is heading in the wrong direction because I am so lost and I have given up on hope. Spencer smiled at me and then laughed.

Spencer says, "Hearing your sad story makes my life seem a little bit better. I am just kidding with you brother. Listen I have done a lot of things I am not proud of. I am headed to hell because of it. No matter what I do I feel like my end result is hell. This trip is not an eye opener for me, or a wakeup call. I know I can make up for what I have done, or change the past. I am going on this journey just to see when I die where I will be laying my head to rest at.

Brother you should thank your lucky stars that you are even getting the opportunity to reunite with someone that you love. I am going to ride through hell looking at soul's burn in hell. The funny part is in a few I will be back down here to join them and this time it will be for good. I don't need to see it to know that I am going to end up here if I don't change my ways. You can't teach an old dog new tricks and I am not the learning type."

Everything you see here is made to keep people that don't know about this place in the dark. The world isn't ready for what Heaven and Hell has in store for it. If everyone in the world knew about this set up it would be total chaos. The government would try to regulate it and other would oppose it. People fear what they don't understand and destroy things when they feel intimidated.

I have been on this here rodeo 5 times and I feel like I am a veteran. Things are set up to look like we are tourist or going to a convention. No one questions this and no one cares. People don't ask questions when things are starring them right in the face, so since things look like it fits, then people allow these events to go on for centuries."

I can't believe something like this could go unnoticed. I guess if you didn't pay close attention to what was really going on, then you wouldn't have a clue to want was really happening right under your nose. This is right out in the open, and for the people that aren't involved is clueless. With all of this new found knowledge I didn't notice that we were about to leave.

The bus started to pull out of the park as the bus was completely filled. The bus was a Coach bus that said Go Chicago, and had every single team that you could name on the bus representing Chicago. I told Spencer God must be a Chicago fan because there is Chicago teams' logo all over this bus.

Spencer laughed again and said, "It is all in your mind, they show you whatever city logos that makes you feel comfortable. God has put everything in the image of

what your mind has deemed as your happy place.
Everything is put into place to make you feel at ease and at home.

I didn't t care it was still cool to see something like that especially since I was heading into the alternate universe that quite frankly scared the crap out of me. I was starting to loosen up a little bit and relax.

Spencer seemed to know a lot about what was going on, but it was something about him I didn't like. Spencer stood 6'2 and he was a very muscular guy. He had tattoos all over his arms. If I saw him on the street I would have thought he was one of Hell's Angels. My mother always told me that if someone seems too good to be true, then they usually are.

Growing up as a kid I was the kid that no one wanted to mess with. For the first time I felt out of place. I didn't know where I was going, or what I got myself into. I was afraid of what was to come, and at this point all I wanted was to run into my mother's arms.

I didn't know if I could trust this guy or not, so I kept my guard up. Spencer and I were there for different reasons. I really wasn't paying too much attention to why he was there, or what he has been through. I was just trying to take everything in and to make sense of what was going on.

All of a sudden out of nowhere it started to rain but only in one spot and that was the entrance way into Crossroad Park. At the entrance way there is an arch way made of metal bars that has Crossroad Park engraved in stone at the stop of the structure. The rain started to get intense as we slowly approached the entrance way.

Then all of a sudden the bus pushed it full speed ahead as it passed through the Arch way. In this world everything was literally gray. Everyone looked exactly the same. It was a world that I wasn't accustomed to, but a world that I will never forget. I was partnered up with Spencer who other than him going to hell seemed like a cool guy now. I was judging him on who I thought he was, and not on his actions. Who am I to judge someone? I don't know what he went through in his life, so I will give him a chance to prove me wrong.

They gave us room keys until the bus that will take us to our final destination arrives. It was surprising because the rooms looked a lot like hotels on earth except it showed us how it would be like living in heaven or hell on the television in our rooms. We weren't allowed to leave the building, or even leave our rooms until we were told to do so.

There were guards roaming the halls to stop us from leaving, but it was for our safety. We were all warned that there are demons that try to snatch humans out of Limbo, and into hell. Room service came, and gave us meals. Maybe this trip will be good for me.

Even though I felt that this place has some similarities to earth, it almost felt like something was missing. I had to be aware of my surroundings because I wasn't at home anymore. If this wasn't a dream, then I had to make sure that I made it back in one piece.

Spencer said, "He never enjoyed his trips, but it's something he had to mentally get himself ready for if he wanted to survive the time that he will spend in hell. The big tough guy after talking to him for a while seems more like a harmless kitten. I guess you can't judge a book by its cover.

He started to cry and breakdown. The man that seemed confident in showing total disregarded for the purpose of his trip. He was now showing signs that it did matter to him that he was going to hell. I don't know if what bothered him the most was going to hell, or not knowing if he would make it out alive. Spencer asked me if

I could give him a towel to wipe his face off out of the bathroom.

I left my ticket and my baseball cap on my bed, and went to the bathroom. I didn't think about what I had done until I returned from the bathroom. When I came back into the bedroom my ticket and Spencer were gone. On the bed were Spencer's ticket, and my baseball cap with a note beside it.

The note said: *I am so sorry Mike for doing this to you, but I couldn't bare another trip to hell. I know that you will be strong enough to get out of hell, but I feel that I needed to see for myself if I could have a chance to be a part of heaven's world. I am truly sorry for what I have done, and don't know if God will let me in after what I have done, but I needed to see heaven for myself before my judgment day comes that will probably now send me to hell. Again I am truly sorry; Sincerely Spencer.*

Chapter 3

I started to panic, and then I ran down the hall screaming my ticket to heaven has been stolen. Then Paul announced over the PA system the buses to heaven and hell are now boarding. I ran as fast as I could to the bus going to heaven, and Paul wasn't there it was a guy named Joseph. Joseph said to me can I see your ticket. I told Joseph that there is a guy named Spencer on this bus who has stolen my ticket to heaven. I told him that he left behind his ticket to hell for me. Joseph said, "Is there anyone by the name of Spencer on this bus? "

Joseph was the bus driver that is going to take everyone to and from heaven. I was starting to realize that I couldn't trust anyone, but I had at this point to put my trust in someone. Joseph was an older man and of average height. Nothing major stood out about him other than his eyes. When I looked into his eyes I saw truth, loyalty and love. But since Spencer stole my ticket I didn't know what to think anymore.

So, there I stood again lost. I felt as though I didn't deserve any happiness or answers. I wasn't on earth anymore, but it felt as if I never left. This moment in time may have changed me forever without me even realizing it. How many times can something go wrong before a person realizes nothing will ever go right?

Joseph was my only hope and I was depending on him to help me make things right. My life and my existence were in his hands. I chose to put all of my trust in him because I didn't want to be stuck in Limbo, or somehow in hell. I took a leap of faith, so I hope I didn't jump into the pit of doom.

I needed to get back on this bus. When I find Spencer I will make him pay. For now I need to get on this bus. No matter what happens I can't let this bus leave without me. They have to let me on this bus. Dad if you are watching please don't let this bus leave with!

We looked around and no one answered. I screamed Spencer I know you are on this bus, so do the right thing, and give me back my ticket. Spencer didn't answer, and Joseph wouldn't let me search the bus. Joseph told me that the bus has to leave, and that I will have to produce a ticket or get off the bus. I got off the bus knowing that Spencer screwed me. I thought he was a nice guy who has made bad decisions in his life, but deserved a second chance. But now I felt that he was worst then the devil himself. I felt betrayed by not only society, but God as well.

Joseph looked at me and said, "I am truly sorry, but without a ticket you are not allowed on this bus. I don't have a list of who should and shouldn't be on this bus. All I do is collect the tickets as they board. So if Spencer is on this bus he isn't saying anything.

I ran through the bus against the bus driver's permission. I looked through the trash can and looked at everyone staring back at me like I was insane as I made my way to the back of the bus. There was no Spencer, so I checked the last place he could be. I checked the restroom, and again no Spencer. Spencer wasn't on the bus or in the restroom. Where could Spencer have gone? Why would he steal my ticket and not use it? Now I am confused and devastated at the same time.

Joseph looked at me and said, "I am sorry but I am about to leave. You are going to have to get off this bus. I will see what I can do when I reach heaven, but for now I am going to have to ask you to get leave. I hope everything works out for you and you find what you are looking for."

So, reluctantly I got on the bus going to Hell where Paul was the driver. I told Paul that a guy named Spencer had stolen my ticket, and he assured me that I would be going to heaven after he dropped off the people going to hell. But I thought that the trip was on the bus, and that no one was allowed to get off?

Paul said, "This time around the rules are a little didn't. Everyone has to go through pain to find their way to true happiness. So, God wanted them to see up close and personal what an eternity in hell would feel like if they didn't change their ways. I know it seem a little excessive and cruel. But you have to understand that if they know that they are in a safe place, then seeing it would not make them believe in the purpose of this trip. They have to believe that this could be their path if changes aren't made."

So, what if none of them makes it out? What if everyone who goes on this trip is trapped in hell? Will God be ok with sacrificing his children to prove a point? No journey is worth getting killed over. I would rather go on living without knowing certain things; then to be trapped for eternity in a place I don't belong.

Paul smiled and said, "God loves all his children. You have faith in God because no matter what you do or where you are God is always there. No one is trapped in hell as long as they keep their faith in God. So, people in God, and trust that with him by yourself you can get through anything even hell. As for you this is not your trip, and not the path for you to take. Under no circumstances are you to get of this bus. Let everyone get off the bus, and when it is time for me to pick them up I will. You will stay on this bus until you reach heaven. Do you understand me Michael?"

I understand under no circumstances was I to get off the bus or I will have to stay my remaining of my journey in hell like everyone else. So, what will happen to Spencer? Paul said, "That Spencer will be allowed in heaven and will have to face the ones he loves knowing that he got in by committing a sin.

He will have to face his family, and look into their eyes as he begs for their forgiveness. You on the other hand Michael will be reunited with your father before you know it; it is going to just take a little bit longer than you anticipated. Remember no matter what do not get off this bus."

Paul seemed like a guy that would give you the shirt of his back. He understood the situation that I was in. He wore shades, so I couldn't see Paul's eyes. Paul was an older guy and he almost seems as if he could have been my grandfather. I felt as though I was in the presence of a very wise man.

Paul started telling jokes and told me how life was when he was growing up. Paul was the middle child who grew up with eight siblings. His father died before he was born and his Mom worked two jobs. I felt a connection with Paul and at that moment I didn't feel so bad for what I was going through.

It is sad how someone else's problems can make you reflect on your own. It wasn't as though I had a break through, or as if Paul's life struggles made mine seem less tragic. I just felt that Paul understood me and I understood him. If this wasn't Paul's full time gig I would love to hear his words of wisdom back home from time to time.

Paul looked at me and said, "You can't always get what you want, but God will always give you what you need. Life is filled with ups and downs. I didn't grow up getting what I wanted. I grew up getting what I needed from my love ones. I never thought anything was promised to me, and I always worked hard to get the things I thought I wanted. Even if it took some time to get something I wanted I knew that eventually my hard work would pay off. With all the materialistic gifts I worked too hard to obtain I really didn't feel in the end made me happy. I would rather try my best to work for something I can believe in than to work hard at something I can do without.

Complaining about what I don't have, what others have, or why I feel cheated solves none of my problems.

You have to remember we all make mistakes. Life is a learning process that end result gets you a sit in heaven. Earth is nothing more than a test that doesn't always have a pass or fail. God is the one that when he calls you to the front of the class will give you your final grade. You can analysis what you did by right and wrong. When it is all said and done God has the final say.

The bus is driving through the entrance of hell that looks like a city in earth that has been hit by poverty. There are pain and suffering all around us and people asking for help. The bus pulls us to what looks like a toll booth, and this guy comes up to the door. The guy says, I am the sheriff of these parts of hell and my name is Judas. I will take over from here. The people on the bus who was chosen to go into hell all got off the bus as planned, and walked across the line and was all chained to one another like a chain gang.

The sheriff looked at Paul and then looked at me. Paul said that he's with me and then closed the door. Paul made a u- turn and drove back toward Limbo. I asked Paul who was that guy and why were those people chained together?

Paul looked at me and said, "That Sheriff Judas has been granted power over this part of town where new comers arrive. He doesn't care if you are a lost soul, a sinner, or on a journey like yours Michael. All he cares about is making sure as long as he has you in his possession you are brutally tortured.

There are three parts of hell. The part that we are in is called Hell's breeding ground where people try to prove themselves to Satan. The second part is called the Forest of Burning Souls where souls are sent that failed to please Satan or are God worshipers. The third part is where Satan lives and his followers who have sold their souls to live a life of luxury. Satan knows everything that goes on down here and he doesn't allow kindness or compassion.

You must be as ruthless as the next to survive down here. No one is safe not even Sheriff Judas who has to be on guard for someone waiting to take his place. You can't die in hell, but your soul can burn for an eternity in the Forest of Burning Souls. In Hell's breeding ground you can try to hide, or wait until a bus like I have to come through. But there are creatures all around us that will stop at nothing to keep you here, and to please their master. So, why aren't these creatures trying to stop us from getting out? It's just the two of us and we could easily be taken out?

Are they just toying with us to see if we will panic trying to get out? Paul smiled, and told me that this is God's bus, and they may not like me, but they fear God. You mean to tell me that since this is God's bus they will let us pass. Paul smiled again and said the glory of God is powerful and nothing can stop it. I thought to myself it does matter as long as I get out of here. I smiled back at Paul and said next stop Heaven!

We pulled up to a gas station and Paul told me that he had to make a quick stop. He went inside convenient store that only had one small window by the cashier. I thought to myself if this is a bus of God shouldn't it run without gas? Paul told me to stay on the bus and no matter what don't get off. Paul went in the store, and for some reason it is taking him a long time to come out.

I didn't understand what was going on. Things felt out of place and I felt that I was having a nightmare. I am in hell and the driver stops at a gas station for gas. I didn't see any more buses or cars here. The pumps didn't have anything to pump the gas out with. So, why were we here? How were we going to get gas?

Who in the hell gets gas in hell? I couldn't figure

out if this was really happening, or if I was imagining it all.

Did he pay the man and what type of money did he use?

Does heaven have a gas station as well and their own

money? At this point I gave up on what was real, and what

was a part of my imagination. All I wanted was to finish

this trip and get back home where I know what I can trust is

real.

While he's in the gas station something strange is

going on outside the bus across the street. There is a little

girl being dragged into a building by her hair. She looks

like she's no more than 8 years old and extremely terrified

of the thing dragging her. She was being dragged by a big

buffed guy in a trench coat with a hood covering his face. I

started to knock on the window of the bus trying to get

Paul's attention, but he never looked my way. I don't think

he could hear me, and I felt like I needed to do something.

For some reason I pushed the back door open. I ran across the street and picked up a crowbar that was lying on the curb. I ran up the stair and into the building shouting LET THE GIRL GO, LET THE GIRL GO YOU DIRT BAG! I heard the young girl screaming PLEASE SOMEBODY HELP ME; PLEASE CAN SOMEBODY HELP ME. I got to the door, and it was locked. The guy yelled back GO AWAY AND LET ME FINISH WHAT I STARTED!

I kicked in the locked door, and on the bed were two hell beasts. So, I ran fast as I can down the stairs, and out the door. The beasts were biting at the heels of my shoes, but I didn't look back as I fell down the bottom steps. I got up, and started to swing the crowbar. When I looked up the beasts was gone; it was like they vanished into thin air. I arrived outside, and to my demise the bus was gone. Paul had left me behind; he has abandoned me. He left me for dead and to fend for myself.

WHY DIDNT I JUST LISTEN TO HIM? NOW I AM STUCK IN HELL! GOD I DON T DESERVE TO BE HERE! I WAS FINALLY GOING TO BE REUNITED WITH MY FATHER, AND THIS IS HOW I AM TREATED! THIS IS NOT WHAT I SIGNED UP FOR NOW GET ME OUT OF THIS HELL HOLE!

No one answered me and I kept on repeating to myself why did I get off this bus a million times. My joyous trip turned into a living nightmare. What was I to do; and where was I to go? I was stuck in hell, and the only way out is to wait for the others to leave. What if the bus never comes back, and where do I go to get on another bus? WHY DID I GET OFF THE BUS? PULL YOURSELF TOGETHER. THERE IS NO TIME TO PANIC. YOU MUST THINK OF AWAY TO GET OUT OF HERE!

I stood in the middle of the road motionless, and not knowing which way to go. No matter which way I went its hell all around me. I didn't really notice a lot of things while I was on the bus, but the atmosphere fear in hell is dark. I don't mean dark in a sense that its pit black, but it has a red sun, gray clouds and a sky that looks like it is on fire. The trees are black, and the leaves look dead. The building are all run down. There are churches on every corner with a six point stop on the door; I am guessing it's the symbol of the devil. The street as far as I can see doesn't have a soul on it except mine.

What's that noise? I turn around, and it's an officer in a patrol car. I hope this isn't who I think it is. If this is Sheriff Judas then my days in surviving is hell is gone. Sheriff Judas got out of his patrol car with a smirk on his face. I ran as fast as I could, and then out of nowhere hell beasts started chasing me. It looked like hundreds of them coming after me. I kept running as fast as I could, but they were gaining on me.

They all surrounded me in the alley like lions hunting down their prey. They were ready to devour me and rip apart my fresh, but Sheriff Judas like Moses parted the sea of beasts trying to destroy me. He had sent the beasts to do his dirty work, and capture me.

He threw me to the ground and said you are coming with me porch monkey. I said what if I don't want to come with you? He laughed and said if you don't porch monkey my friends will eat you alive and then dump your soul in a river of fire to burn for an eternity. He yelled out, "NOW GO PORCH MONKEY." He kept repeating that over and over as we walked back to his car. I got in the back sit, and he began to explain what hell is waiting for me as he drove away laughing.

Porch monkey I knew there was something about you when I saw you on that bus that I didn't like. You are just like the rest of the porch monkeys I have come across; you are think that you all are something special; but you're not. You thought your people knew what slavery was; well you haven't experience real slavery yet. You can thank your God for leaving you down here because what happens here on out is his doing. I don't care what color you are, and if it was up to me the entire human race would have been enslaved.

Now look here porch monkey I am going to drop you off into the next town, and if you survive the night I would be surprised. A little heads up for you porch monkey we likes to hunt at night, so if you see any of your friends hiding out let them know we like all types of meat. SO, UNTIL THEN GET OUT OF MY CAR PORCH MONKEY! He threw me out of the car about three miles away from the exits out of hell into a town that looks unoccupied, so I walked around. I saw bars, churches, restaurants, apartment buildings and stores that all looked empty.

Chapter 4

Hell looked and felt like hopelessness. I could smell burning fresh in the air. When the wind blows it cuts your soul. For every good thought I had my body started to burn as if hell knew I didn't belong here. It started to rains and it felt like acids and your body feels like it's been cooked. I don't why this was happening, but I had to find shelter fast. Now I feel helpless, and I feel like the only way to survive was to run and hide. Someone grabbed me from behind.

The guys told me to be quiet, or they will get us. I can help you but you have to trust me. If you follow me I can get you to safety, food, clothes, and a chance to live another day. I didn't know if I could trust him, but I didn't have any other choice. He had some type of shield to protect us from the burning rain. It seemed like we were running forever, but we ended up in this building that looked like a hotel. It was abandoned and ruined down, but it was filled with people like me.

I started to look around the building as the guy told me to make myself at home. Soon as I sat down a lady from a distance stood up, and waved me to come over to her. The guy smiled and said, "We will get a chance to talk later, so go see what the lady wants."

Before I could introduce myself this woman gave me a hug. She stood up at about 5'8 with an athletic build. She was a very beautiful woman, and almost made me forget that I was minutes away from being boiled to death in the burning rain. She introduced herself to me.

She says, "Hi I am Mary, and you are?" I stated "I am Michael." Mary says, Nice to meet you Michael. I see you met Daniel, but before you go meeting everyone else I wanted you to know that you are not alone. We all are here to help each other though whatever this is. To better understand why we are here I will tell you how I got here.

I was a part of the 1992 Volleyball Olympic for USA. I received a gold medal and I won a lot of tournaments. I played professional for the California Sun Sharks. I can remember the day and moment I was taken down here. The only thing that I can think about is how I can get out of here. I have a place, a purpose, and a reason to go on living. This is not the end for me, but another change that I have to overcome.

It was 1994 I had just finished my tournament and my car had a flat tire. A man pulled beside me in a black Mercedes asking me if I needed help. I told him that I was fine and that I had already called AAA. But the guy was persistent and got out of his car. He told me that he knew a guy close by with a tow truck and that he would give me a left to the tow truck place to get my tire replaced.

The rain was coming down and I was tired. As the man approached me I felt this overwhelming attraction to him and didn't want to be anywhere else but with him. The tow truck came and the man took me back to the tow truck place as he promised. The tire was replaced and the man in the black Mercedes asked me out for dinner. Immediately said yes!!!

We had dinner at his place and I couldn't think about the meal or my surroundings. All I could think about was him ripping off my clothes and being inside of me. After about an hour of eating and drinking wine we started having sex in his bed. The room felt as though it was spinning and I kept on yelling don't stop!!!

The next thing I remember is falling asleep in his arms, but when I open my eyes later that night I was in hell. I found myself in the middle of the road naked with no one to help me. I was the first one taken from earth that didn't sell their soul to the devil and as you can see I wasn't the last. It felt as though I was down here alone forever until Daniel and Amy arrived. Everyone else started to join us later in groups."

The guy who pulled me said, "My name is Daniel and we are all escapees of Sheriff Judas. I was once a cop in New York and I got shot in the chest. I was sent to the hospital in critical condition. I was slipping in and out of consciousness. See each time I did that I would go to Limbo and then back to earth.

But when you go to Limbo there are demons that will try to snatch your soul, so they can take it back to hell. The doctor and nursing staff kept on trying to revive me, but I was gone for no more than a minute when a demon pulled me from Limbo after going back and for about 10 minutes. I was sent to hell even before I could get judged by God. I was a good cop, a good husband, father and person I didn't deserve this.

The last thing I can remember before I was snatched from Limbo was one raining day on earth in New York City I was patrolling my normal beat when I approached a black Mercedes with its emergency lights on in the middle of the road. It had to be around 1 am in the morning because there wasn't another vehicle in sight. In that area during rush hour traffic is a mess. The guy approaches my car as I approached his vehicle and said, "I have a flat officer; I could really use a hand changing my tire." I got out my patrol car and helped him changed his tire.

The guy smiled at me and I smiled back at him. As I looked into his eyes I felt like I couldn't turn away. This man had a hold on me and I didn't want him to let go. Sexual images stared flashing before my eyes. Before I could speak the guy kissed me and asked me to come with him. I got in his car with no hesitation. We arrived back at my place. I took out my keys and dropped them. He picked up my keys and told me not to be nervous.

The next thing I know we were having sex and rough sex at that. We kept throwing each other across the room as the sex intensified. We he put his massive penis inside me I instantly felt like I pure bliss. I am a straight man, but I started to feel confused and curious.

At that moment I felt like I was having the best sex of my life. When I had the opportunity to return the favor and put my manhood in him I did until he couldn't take it anymore. We both kept screaming out each other names and asking for more. When it was all said and done he left. I woke up the next morning confused and questioning my sexuality. Was I gay, bi- sexual, or just curious?

The next morning I went to go back and get my patrol car and it was gone. I couldn't go back to work without my car or call it in. I would be laughed out the department if I reported my patrol car stolen. I decided to wait until 1 am and hoped maybe my car would turn up like the man did. Maybe he took my car and wanted to bring it back to me so he could see me again. I started to feel sick when I started to think about what I did last night and didn't feel that same attraction I did before.

All of a sudden I fell to my knees and hit the ground. I felt pain coming from my chest. I had been shot from behind. My life started to flash before my eyes. I tried to hold on and I remember being put into an ambulance. I heard the paramedic say, "Hold on we are going to get you to the hospital. Hang in there Sir you are going to make it! Stay with me Sir!" When I arrived at the hospital I tried to fight for my life, but something on the other side had plans for me.

A lady in the back stood up who looked as though she could be my mom and started telling me her story. Hi my name is Amy and as Mary has already said I arrived here shortly after Daniel did. I use to do drugs and I met this guy online that said he had some good dope that would blow my mind. Who was I to say no? When you are hooked on the stuff your next fix can come from anywhere. I didn't care who, where, or how I got it. As longs as I can scratch that itch, then I was happy. We all have things in our past that we wished we could take back.

So, I invited him over my house. He seemed cool for a few weeks and then things started to change. He gave me this tablet that had some kind of liquid in it. He called it Liquid Paradise. He said that it was going to hit the streets in a matter of days and that I was the first one other than him to try it. I told him that I wasn't sure that it was safe and I told him to leave. He told me that he was sorry and that he wanted to make it up to me. I said ok and he said that he wanted to make me dinner.

So, I let him in my kitchen. He cooked sea bass, carrots, baked potatoes, cheesecake and we had red wine. Everything was going good until I drunk the wine. I didn't realize that he had put the liquid paradise in my drink until it was too late. He laughed at me and told me that he would see me in hell. I woke up and I was in Limbo, and he was there waiting for me.

I had just finalized my divorce with my husband and I found myself attracted to him. I was a shy person, but something about him was making me desire him. I started to have thoughts that I would normally find disgusting. For the first time I felt like I wanted him to ravish my whole body, but instead I was tricked. I later found out that he had the power to make anyone of the flesh desire him.

It turns out the guy was Sheriff Judas and he's been preying on lost souls for centuries. I tried to run and I kept on calling on God for help, but there was no answer. He threw me in a cell and said that you will be raped every single day. My guards and I will take turns with you until we break your soul. One day a guard came in and instead of me hiding in a corner I greeted him with a smile. I pulled down his pants and started performing oral sex. Tears fell down my cheeks and I started to gag a little. But I knew what I had to do, so I bit down hard as I could on the guard's penis. He started to bleed, and I ran out the cell with blood dripping from my mouth. I ran as far as I could and hid in this building.

I can't tell you what day or year it is. The last thing I remember is it was about to be the year 2000. Don't know what is out there and I don't plan on finding out. Once you get away from someone like that you don't ever want to be in their presence ever again. Sheriff Judas is out there and the only thing that will make me take a step out there is if God sent a rescue party. Mary and Daniel are warriors and we all depend on them for over survival.

I am not going to tell you to give up hope my child, but you should start calling this place home. Daniel and Mary tries to help those that they can, but it's not much anyone could do being good souls in hell."

So, you mean to tell me that we will never get out of here? What about the bus Paul said that there is a bus that comes through her to pick up people after their journey is over. They all looked at me in disbelief.

Daniel stood up and said, "That there is no bus. The guy you are referring to probably worked for Sheriff Judas and they tricked you." That can't be right I said. Paul was going to take me to heaven, but I got off the bus. He told me not to get off the bus and I did because I thought I saw someone in need of help.

Daniel was a white male standing at about 5' 9 and had a naval seal tattoo on his left arm. He seemed to be a straight forward and a no nonsense type of guard. I felt that if anyone could get us out of here it was him. I felt that I had to keep a watchful eye on everyone and everything since I didn't know if someone was trying to deceive me. I didn't know if I could trust Daniel, but I guess in time I would find out.

I have been betrayed by Spencer, and Paul left me to die in hell. At this point trusting people wasn't an option for me. I am no one's fool, so these people here are all my enemies. Until I can find out if I have any friends I will trust no one.

How could an ex-cop and naval seal let his guard down? I felt like I was the only one ready to leave this place. Daniel seemed too calm and didn't think that it was any hopes of leaving. He went on and on about how he's a survivor. This man talked the talk, but I still was trying to figure out where he was trying to walk the walk to.

I am sorry for what happen, but what happened to you was the work of Satan. He will do and go through all types of measures to get goods soul here. They want to see good souls burn in hell for an eternity and demons will be rewarded tremendously for the amount of good souls that they bring to hell to please their Lord Satan. There was never a trip, journey, or a bus that was going to take you to heaven. This was all the work of Satan to get you here. I am truly sorry."

I can't be stuck here; there has to be a way out. I have family and friends to go back too. This can't be how it all ends for me? I wasn't a perfect person, or a saint. I know I don't deserve to be here. Daniel said, "None of us deserve to be here and we all have family that we miss back on earth."

I DON' T CARE HOW LONG IT TAKE, BUT I WILL FIND A WAY OUT OF HERE! So, what do we do for food and water? Mary said, "Well since we are in hell we can't starve to death, so we hunt. We will hunt the hell beasts while they sleep at night. The beast feast on fear and weak souls and they travel in packs. They hunt during the day and roam the treat as Sheriff Judas patrol searching for something for them to snack on. He usually leaves us alone, but if we piss him off, or try to find a way out the beast will have us for dinner."

You said that you all hunt, so where are your weapons? Daniel and Mary who I am guessing are the leaders took me to the back room where it was filled with weapons that I don't think came from earth. What is this, and where did you get all of this?

There were machetes, knifes, swords and other little things that looked useless to me. I thought how they were going to win a fight against hell with all this crap. The groups seemed proud that they were able to get this stuff, but I didn't want to rain on their parade knowing that we didn't have a fighting chance.

So, I lied and I pretended to care. If their hopes were to be crushed it wasn't going to be by me; it was going to be by the hands of hell. Daniel said, "We had a guy working for us on the inside. He had to commit some horrific act to get them to trust him. In order to get close to Sheriff Judas or Satan one must display total disregard for others.

A person must show that they are the strongest, and kill those that stand in their way. So, John went to Sheriff

Judas with two men who he gave as a sacrifice to them to prove his loyalty. It was two guys that Sheriff Judas couldn't find, and wanted to kill. Sheriff Judas was pleased, and made John his right hand man. John had to bury his good soul deep down inside, so he wouldn't be found out.

So, every time Sheriff Judas left for earth or Limbo John would bring us some much needed supplies back. This was going on for months and going well until Satan told Sheriff that he had a trader amongst them. John was quickly founded out when he refused to kill a little girl that Satan stole from Limbo. He was tortured in the middle of the street for all to see and we were all told that are day will come. Now John's body will rest in the Forest of Burning Souls where unfortunately he will burn for an eternity. Satan knows all down here, but he only cares about us being here when he's being made a fool of, he wants us all to live here for an eternity in fear. By killing us off one by one he takes away the little hope that we have left. "

Chapter 5

I know firsthand how it feels for your hope to be crushed. I can't believe this is our only option. I came here for a reason, and now I have to fight just to stay alive. This isn't my fight, but I guess no one else signed up for this either.

When I got here Sheriff Judas took the people on the bus into a building on the other side of town. Why did he take them in that building and what does this all mean? Mary told me that maybe he wanted me to think that he was torturing souls there. And maybe you felt so guilty about not helping them that you reacted by impulse by trying to help what you thought was a little girl.

So, you mean to tell me all this was a game of cat and mouse? IF I EVERY GET MY HANDS ON SHERIFF JUDAS YOU MARK MY WORDS HE WILL PAY!

I want to join your team and help you all. I figure while I am here I should at least make a difference. This is not what I had envisioned when I wanted to help fight the good fight. I don't know if I will live to see tomorrow, but what I do know is I will go out fighting. So, what do we do first? Tell me what I need to do to help, and I will help. And Daniel thanks for helping me back there. I don t know what would of happened if I continued to run. Thank you, I will never forget what you done for me. Let's get down to busy they said.

Mary said, "We patrol in groups at sunrise and we leave one group behind to hold down the fort. We have survived down here for so long because we are efficient, and work as a unit. We try to catch the beast while they are sleeping, and surround the first one we see because there will not be another opportunity to kill another once one wakes up. We don't leave anyone behind, and we don't get greedy. We take what we can when we can, and we comeback. We travel on foot, and we always stay together. Do you have any questions?"

Were you in the military? You sound as though you are drafting me to be in the army. She smiled at me and said, "I was on the volleyball team in high school. I use to hang out with some of my friend who had ROTC in high school, but it wasn't for me. Even though I wasn't in the army I had plenty of brothers that were in the army. Being the only girl with five brothers I was taught how to fight at an early age. I was at the top of my martial arts class that I took when I spent six months in Japan with my International Volley Ball Team. They said that I was a natural fighter and born leader. When people started to recognize me for my talents in volleyball I became cocky and arrogant. I had the world in the palm of my hand. Whatever I wanted and desired I could get without even having to ask for it. The world was mine and I knew it.

I started to hang out with the wrong crowd when I came back from winning the gold medal and I got hooked on heroin. When my family founded out I was called a disgrace and no one respected me after that. I started to head down a dark path that eventually lead me here."

I am sorry to hear that, but at least you are doing some good in these people that you helped saved lives. I don't know what I would of done if Daniel didn't pull me in here. Don't worry will we find a way out of here. Even if we don't find a way out of here we can all give them hell trying to stop us. This might sound strange, but for the first time in my life I feel like I am a part of a greater good, and I have you all to thank for that. They told me that the beast sleeps at nightfall and so are the beasts that roam the streets during the day with Sheriff Judas his pets?

They all hide in the basement which is made like a safe haven from a bomb attack. Every sunrise the creatures of hell bring chaos to this part of town to find any remaining souls that doesn't want to worship Satan, and are too weak to be one his followers. It's a few minutes until the sun comes up, and I can see the horrified looks on their faces. Mary and Daniel shouts out EVERYONE TO THE BASEMENT NOW! Everyone heads to the basement, and chains the door close. There is a rumbling sound going on outside, and crawling. You can feel the evil presence blowing passed like the wind. The presence was, so strong that it almost destroyed what good I had left in me. The ground was trembling like it was an earthquake.

When the sunset everyone outside were all gone; it was peaceful for at least the moment. Daniel, Mary and I went to the top of the stairs holding machetes. Daniel ran got to the top first swinging his machete. He screamed out, "They destroyed everything!" The chairs, blankets, and cots that they have also stolen from Satan were all destroyed. Everything that they tried to accomplish was wiped out overnight. I don't believe it was Sheriff Intent to destroy us; I believe his intent was to destroy our hopes of survival.

It was now clear that this was a battle that they cannot win, and by the looks on their faces I knew that the end was near. No longer was there hope in the air, it was only despair. No one said a word, but it was clear to me that I had to luck out for myself. I didn't want to make things worse, so I started to pick up the broken chairs, and the rest of them followed my lead.

Everyone were just cleaning up for the rest of the day, and by night fall we all stayed at the top waiting for them to come take us because we all knew it was just a matter of time. No one came that night it was peaceful at least for one night. We all went into the streets not caring if this was a trap or not. Everyone in the town who was all hiding out in building in this center part of the town. I thought what was so special about this part, and why did Sheriff Judas drop me off here? Everyone started talking, and hugging each other as though it was all over.

All I wanted to know is why us and why here?

Daniel said that we all needed to get back inside and we all need to work together. Daniel was right, and so that is what we all did. We all gathered in the building that was previously a harvest building for the beast that took their meat that they devoured. There was blood, rotting fresh, bones, and corpses everywhere. Their souls were gone, and their bodies were left behind for us to find. They wanted to send us a message, and let us know that at any time we could be next. There were at least 100 dead bodies in one room alone.

There were bodies of kids, the elderly, pregnant women, men and women of all ages. We went up the stairs to the top floor of the building that looked like it hasn't been touched. It looked like it was the office of the president, or someone powerful.

Each room was over crowded, but it looked like the size of the Presidential Hotel back in Chicago. It was huge enough to fit all of us and then some. It was beginning to become clear to all of us that this too might be a set up. They have all of us in the town in one building like sitting ducks. They could all just storm the building, and destroy us all. I said I don't trust them, or anyone for that matter. I told them that we all should watch our backs because they could have sent spies. I sounded paranoid and a little crazy, but the truth was hard to deal with. I couldn't think outside of the box. I was worried about my survival.

We are at war Mary shouted across the room, so we better start acting like it. We started moving this from the other building that wasn't destroyed from the other night into the new building we now called home. I didn't know what time it was, what day it was, and I was started to forget what year it was. Everything I had held dear to me on earth was slipping away and being replaced by constant fear. All I could think about was being devoured, and having my soul burn forever. Not only did I have to worry about the hell beast, but there were also humans that sold their souls to Satan. These people were cannibals and God knows what else is out there. So, we all gathered in a big run below the floor we all settled in at, and we talked about how to survive.

Everyone wanted to be the boss, and everyone thought their ideas was better than the other person shouting across the room. Everyone was hiding out from the evil that surrounding them on this part of town and no one wonder why. So, I shouted out DOES ANYTHING CARE WHY THEY WOULD LET US LIVE, AND LEAD US ALL HERE TO FIND THIS BUILDING? I DONT CARE ABOUT ALL YOUR STUPID IDEAS, AND I THINK IT'S ABOUT TIME THAT WE STARTED THINKING OF WAYS TO GET OUT OF HELL! The room became silent, and everyone stared at me for a while.

Daniel said, "He is right we need to find a way to get out of here and not just a way to survive." I said the only way to survive is to get out of here and at least make it back to Limbo. We need to get to the main gate if we have any chance of survival. I think I still remember the way to get there out of here. I was paying attention to where I was running, and what direction Sheriff Judas was taking me in. If we all make a run for it they can't catch us all. Some of us might not make it, but I think that is a chance we have to take.

This wasn't the hell that I had envisioned, or was told about growing up. I was looking for a much darker, and a hell that would torture me for an eternity. Hell was more like earth to me, but in here we all assumed we knew who were evil and good. The streets, the buildings, and the human beings all look as though it was plucked from earth and put here. Hell seemed too peaceful, and felt a lot like home to me. I didn't understand why hell would show mercy on us, and why hell wasn't as horrific as I wanted it to be. Everyone started to set up battle stations just in case

Sheriff Judas and the rest of the demonic creatures came back. Everyone took turns as the days went on hunting for food, and watching out. I think it has been over a couple of years now since I been here, but I am not too sure because time doesn't exist down here.

Amy walked over to my table where I was cleaning my weapon. Mary Ann says, "I see something in you that I don't see in all the rest, so I think I can trust you. See everyone here believes there will come a time when someone will come save us. But with ever soul that arrives here their hopes becomes a little thinner each moment as time passes. I can see within you is the heart of a man that will put everyone on his shoulders and lead them all out of here. I have been here for a long time and I keep to myself. Just because I don't say anything doesn't mean I don't know what goes on down here. When the time comes you will know what to do Michael. I have faith in you and you should have faith in yourself as well."

Mary and Daniel looked over at my table. I could see that they were both wondering what was going on. It is like they were the sergeants and we were the privates' goofing off. They didn't look too happy seeing Amy at my table socializing. I guess I couldn't blame them. Stress in hell was at this point at an all-time high and what we were planning to do next would take a lot of planning. If we all were going to get out of here, then we all had to make sure everything was planned out to the very last detail.

Now that Amy had walked away from my table and went back to her area I started to think if there were traders among us. Was Amy trying to get inside my head by trying to form an alliance with me and later betraying me? Could Amy simply be trying to let me know to be aware of my surrounding and be careful who I trust?

We went on a few more practice runs and night mission to see if we could pull off this one chance of escaping hell. Because once we reach the gates of hell there was literally no turning back. Amy and I talked a few more times since the first time she reached out to me. If I make it out here alive I would definitely keep in touch with her because she has opened my eyes to a lot of things.

No one was more anxious to leave then me. We all knew what was at stake here and there was no room for error. Everyone had to be alert, focused and willing to do whatever it took to get out safely. No one thought that it would be easy and some thought that not everyone would make it out. We all were taking a big risk trying to escape from hell, but if there was a right time to do so now was it.

Everyone was beginning to think that we were in the clear, and it was time for us to go back home. So, we all gathered up our weapons, and stared heading out the building. Mary, Daniel, and I lead the way. Everyone took a chance and we all started walking down the quiet road at the crack of dawn, and there wasn't a soul out. It seems that we were all going to make it. Limbo was just ahead of us over a hill. But all of a sudden it started to get dark, and we could all see the portal to Limbo shining bright.

We all started to run, but Daniel and Mary said they think it's a trap. We should go around and cut through the alley. So, they all followed them, but I kept on straight ahead. I made it through the portal, and into Limbo. I could hear the other screaming for their lives, it sounded like a massacre out there. I ran through Limbo screaming for Gods help. HELP ME LORD! HELP ME LORD! I turned around and there were Mary and Daniel behind me. I told them to stay away from me. I knew something was up with them, but I didn't t know what. I knew that I couldn't trust them two so I ran as fast as I could. I ran and ran, but I got hit from behind. I woke up a few minutes later and Mary and Daniel were holding me down.

Sheriff Judas was standing there in front of me smiling, "He said, Boy you can't escape hell and there is no way I am going to let you leave." Why are you doing this

Daniel and Mary I thought you both cared about helping others? Mary laughed and said, "The only thing that we care about is pleasing our Lord Satan. I learn years ago when I first arrived here that you must do whatever it takes to survive. I gave up on caring for us back then when I knew no matter what I did to help us it would never make a difference. So, Sheriff Judas came to me first and told me to get as many God worshipers I can together so we could destroy them all in exchange for whatever I desire."

Daniel said, "I met up with Mary like I told you before. But she told me the truth about hell. And she made me realize that the only way out is to destroy the weak. Don't you see kid that there is no way out, and you need to join us before you meet the fate like the others. We told them over the years to stop asking for God to help, but they wouldn't listen. When we met up with the rest of you weak and pathetic souls we knew what needed to be done. Everything we went through they all still believe that their

Lord actually cares about them. Do you actually think kid that your Lord gives a damn about you? The rest of them will be caged like the weak animals that they are, but Sheriff Judas has something special in store for you."

I started to trust again, and for what? Now I am in deeper than before, and this time I don't think I can get out of this. Back on earth I was the strongest, and people feared me. In hell I was as helpless as my little buddy Andrew. How could I have let this happen? Why didn't I listen to Paul, and stayed on the bus? I had to be a hero, and now looked where it took me.

How can I have been so stupid, and so naïve? If this was the end for then I will not go out without a fight. I pulled Daniel off of me and got his weapon. I pushed Mary to the ground, and I was about to kill them both. But then someone hit me from behind, and I hit the ground. When I woke up I was tied up, and when I looked up I saw Sheriff

Judas. If this is the end for me, then kill me now Sheriff Judas because you will never take my soul.

If I have to burn in hell, then I will burn in hell believe that I fought to the end. So do what you will with my body. Even if my soul burns I know that God will be there with me. So do what you will because you are a coward, and so is your boss.

Chapter 6

Sheriff Judas smiled and then picked me up off the ground. He kicked me in the stomach over and over until I hit the ground again. I fell to the floor and then he punched me in the face over and over until I began to bleed. He kept on saying to me, "WHERE IS YOUR PRECIOUS GOD NOW PORCH MONKEY? WHERE IS YOUR PRECIOUS GOD NOW?" I looked at him straight in the eyes, as I was coughing up blood, and said I know where my God is. So tell me where is your God? He laughed at me, and said do you really think that your God cares about you. I smiled. Does it really matter right now?

Sheriff Judas turned around and told them to hold me up. He punched me in the face over and over again. I passed out and when I woke up this time I was chained to a wall in a dungeon. Across from me in the dungeon was a woman. She was unconscious; she looked like an angel. I was kind of in a daze, but it was clear to me that an angel was sitting across from me. She was saying something to me, but I couldn't t understand her. I was dazed and confused. She repeated, "Are you ok? Are you ok?"

I am ok I guess. I am just a little banged up, but thanks for asking. My name is Michael, and she said her name was Michelle. I smiled and said, "Nice to me you Michelle." She smiled, and said, "You are the first person I have seen in years. They have kept me alone down here it seems like forever."

What did you do and why are you here? Michelle said, "Well I was a good girl at first until I started hanging with the wrong crowd. I started drinking, and doing drugs a lot. I killed my boyfriend because he tried to rape me, but I asked for God forgiveness. I thought I was forgiven, and so I stopped my bad way. I was on the right path. I was going to school, working, and living a normal life. Until one day this drunk driver hit me, and I died on my way to the hospital.

Instead of going to heaven I was in Limbo, and there is where Sheriff Judas snatched me. Sheriff Judas took me to hell, and put me in here. I have been in here ever since. They feed me the fresh of the good, and I have to drink their blood in order to survive. We can't die in hell, but we can suffer for an eternity. I didn't want to suffer anymore. I try holding out on food, and liquids as long as I could but I grew weak. I don't deserve to be here, and I can't believe that God didn't stop him from taking me. Enough about me why are you here?"

Why am I here? I am here because like everyone else I was tricked. But I am now starting to realize that nothing matters anymore. I am going to have to accept the fact that I am stuck here forever, and not fight it. I don't want to be here, but God isn't doing anything to help me get out. I am all alone and promised everyone back there that I would make sure that they got out of hell. I didn't keep my promise and now I feel that this is the end for us all. My family will move on without me soon and I will have to move on as well. I don't like saying this, but in order to survive I think that I have to face the truth.

The truth is if God does not care about me, then why should I? Michelle said with a smile, "Maybe if you do get out one day you should make greeting cards." We both laughed. I told her how I felt all alone on earth. How I use to sit by the phone waiting for one of my friends to call. How I use to hope a pretty lady would walk by and talk to me. I shared my heart and soul with Michelle and for the first time I felt like someone actually cared about what I had to say.

Michelle said, "I have sisters and brother, but I am the oldest. My father is very strict and you have to do things his way. A lot of people fear my father, but he treats me like a princess. I use to spend my free time writing, singing and dancing. I was beginning to think everything was going great in my life until I ended up here. Now I don't know what to believe anymore. All I know now is that I don't know what to believe in anymore.

Maybe you will get out of here someday and maybe you will be able to keep your promise that you made to the others you left behind." Michelle started crying while reminiscing about her past. I couldn't console her because I was chained to the wall across from her. I told her that anything was going to be ok. TIME TO EAT!

A guard comes in and puts one tray by me, and then one tray by Michelle. But instead of leaving the guard he turns around, and starts taking off his pants. He pulls out his penis, and spread Michelle's legs apart. He turns his head and smiles at me. He then turns back around, and starts having sex with Michelle. Michelle cries out STOP; PLEASE STOP!

Twenty minutes later I think passed and the guy gets up and pulls his pants up, and closes the cell. Michelle has her clothes ripped and her lip is bleeding. She has her head down and her hair covering her face. Michelle I will get us out of here. Michelle with her head down says, "Leave me alone please. There isn't anything you can do, so as soon as you can realize this you will know we are stuck here forever."

I screamed for the guard. The guard came and asked me what I wanted. I want you do you the same thing that you did to her to me. Come on you can't tell me that you don't want to have a black man do you? COME AND GET IT!

The same guard bent down in front of me and begins unzipping my pants and then I wrapped my legs around his neck. I squeezed my legs together as tight as I could. He tried to pull my legs a part, but I kept on thinking about what he did to Michelle and squeezed harder. I squeezed harder and harder until he was unconscious. I grabbed his keys off his belt and unchained myself and then I unchained Michelle who looked as though she was in a state of shock. LET GO MICHELLE! SNAP OUT OF IT

WE HAVE TO GET OUT OF HERE!

We got as far as the top stairwell and then Mary and

Daniel was standing there. I hit Daniel in the jaw and

Michelle kicked Mary in the ribs. Daniel and I were

throwing punches until he wrapped a chain around my

neck.

I hit him in the crotch, and then wrapped the chain

around his neck, and twisted until I broke his neck. His soul

came from his body, and went into me. I felt a live, and

powerful. Michelle stabbed Mary with her own knife. Mary

soul went into Michelle. Sheriff Judas came to us as we

were standing there ready for another fight. Sheriff Judas

said, "Now don't you both feel alive now more than ever?

What if I could promise you two an eternity of that, and

more? Work for Satan and you will both enjoy all the

pleasures that hell has to offer. But if you both decline you will enjoy all the pain hell has to offer. Now the choice is yours, so are you guys with us?"

What is it that we would have to do? Why us, and was this all a test? Sheriff Judas smiled at me and said, "You ask too many questions just say yes!" We both said yes and he took us to Satan himself. My heart was beating fast. I didn't know what to expect.

I was meeting Satan not God and I was going to be doing something that goes against everything I stood for. Michelle had a look on her face similar to my own and I knew that we didn't have any other choice. I know that God gave us free will, but what good is free will if you don't have a choice that wouldn't result in your soul burning for an eternity. If I was sacrifice myself to go to heaven I would be all for it. But standing up for myself in hell, so I can burn for an eternity wasn't an option for me.

We approached the gate, and it was a palace. The gate opened up, and there was people all dressed in black standing on the side of our car. I don't know what to think, or even say. As a million thoughts are racing in my mind I felt a connection to Michelle. I looked at Michelle, and she looked back at me. We both didn't say a thing, but we both knew that whatever he had in store for us would change us both forever.

We enter a room that had a fire place, red carpet and black cats the size of lions circling the floor. It was a huge black desk with a huge black chair behind it. There were black sofas and chairs all around the room. They were pictures of God burning all around the room. We were both standing in the middle of the room and then a man appears out of thin air.

He didn't look scary at all, but you can feel the evil inside of him. Part of me was drawn to it, and the other part was terrified. Michelle held my hand tight as we both looked at him. He smiled, and then stared out the window that showed the hell all around us. Satan said, "We live in a time were good and evil are both the same."

You can't tell the difference between good from evil anymore. No longer are people coming to God for guidance, or blessings they are also coming to me. God and I made a deal to see who could get the most humans to follow them. The winner would get earth forever.

So, far God and I are tied. I want earth and then I want heaven. The two of you are going to be my soul collectors and the ones that will help more humans realize they should worship me. Do as you are told and you will live a life of luxury. If you choose to disobey I will take your souls and destroy the souls of everyone you love."

What is it exactly do we have to do? Satan said go to Sheriff Judas, and he will fill you in on the details. We leave Satan and Sheriff Judas is standing down the hall waiting for us. We get to Sheriff Judas and he gives us new clothes to wear. He takes us to two rooms that are a jointed that are fit for a king and queen.

He told us to change our clothes and that we would be eating dinner in the banquet hall in a few hours. Michelle and I stayed in the same room we were afraid to be alone, we have been through so much together. We are dressed up looking as if we should have been walking the red carpet in Hollywood. I have on a tuxedo and she has on a black dress. She looks so beautiful. I am so happy to be with her. She looks at me and smile as she held my hand. Are you nervous? I can't believe we are in hell while we are getting ready to have dinner in the banquet hall with Satan.

She smiles at me and said, "I rather have dinner with him then to be his dinner." We both entered the banquet hall holding hands there are hundreds of humans, demons and creatures of all kinds down here. Everything looks so eloquent. Everything is white and gold. People are walking around serving wine. There was so much to take it. I didn't know where to begin.

There are tables covered in white lace table cloth. Flowers filled the room as if it was a garden. The dance floor was huge floor and on the stage there was a band playing music that made me feel at peace. People playing the violin, guitar, harp, piano, drums and trumpets made it feel like I was in paradise. The music was soothing and I had a moment of clarity.

God has backed me in a corner, and forcing me to choose sides. I didn't want to play any games, and I didn't plan on going to hell. All I wanted was to reunite with me father. All I got in return is a chance to spend an eternity in all. No wonder why good people turn bad, it's because they realized in some point in their lives that being good is a sign of weakness. I don't know who to thank for letting me be with Michelle who is by far the best thing that has ever happened to me. I know that with her here nothing else mattered.

I know that I can burn in hell, but I would be complete with her by my side. Life isn't a life that you live in a home, but the life that you live with someone special that you can go home too. She is my home, my rock and my willingness to live my eternal life in hell.

Michelle looks at me and said, "Michael is everything ok?" I know this is a lot for us to digest, but I think that if we do what we are told we can get through this. I am glad that if I have to spend the rest of my immortal life in hell I am glad it is with you. You are the best thing that has ever happened to me and for that I am thankful for you being here with me. As long as we stick together there is nothing they can do to us."

Michelle kisses me and her lips are soft and her kiss tastes like strawberries. For a moment I forgot where we were. For a moment I realized what true happiness was. For a moment I forgot that I was in hell because her kisses felt like heaven.

We left the part unnoticed and we went back to her room. She started kissing me again and again as she pushes me against her door as we went in. She threw me on the bed and then told me that she wanted to slip into something more comfortable. I am lying on the bed thinking to myself is this really going to happen? Am I going to have sex and am I going to have sex in hell?

Do I have to wear a condom? I don't know what is going on, but what I do know is that I am falling in love with Michelle. Michelle comes out and she is completely naked. She looks at me smiling and says, "So what do you think of my outfit." I smiled back and said that the birthday suit look fits you well. She smiles at me again and sits beside me on the bed.

We are looking into each other eyes. I can feel myself inside of her and we are as one. She is looking deep into my heart and soul. For the first time I feel like I am free. She starts to take my clothes off and our eyes are fixed on one another. She started kissing me and I kissed her back. She lays down on the front of the bed on the silk sheets as I started to kiss her lips. I kissed her lips a thousand times; it was like sweet nectar. Her lips are sweet and juicy like grapes picked from a vine. I kissed her neck; it felt soft against my lips.

As I made my way down I kissed on her nipples ever so gentle with my tongue as I caressed it at the tips. I continued down as I kissed her stomach the home where man kind's future is born. I made my way to the juicy center I kissed her succulent peach until I reached the core.

She screamed out, "Don't stop give me more!" She took her legs from around my waist. She looked at me and said, "Now it's my turn!" She pushed me down on the bed as she works her way from the bottom to the top. She kissed my feet. She kissed my legs with her soft and succulent lips.

She worked her way from my lips to my toe slowly kissing every inch of my body making every second better than the last. She started to gently stroke my manhood and then started stroking it faster. She caressed it with her lip slowly making me forget about the past. I can feel my body ready to burst, but I hold back as she continues to work her way to the top. She kisses my stomach as she makes her way to my chest.

She kisses my nipples with her tongue as then my neck. She kisses my neck as my world is spinning and spinning into a state of complete happiness. She puts her body on top of me, and she is now inside of me. We are connected mind, body, and soul. She is now a part of me, and I am now a part of her.

We stared kissing as tears fall down our faces. We held each other close as our body rocked back and forth like the sea. Nothing made sense, but I knew that this moment was meant to be. I felt like time stood still for us, and we could stay in that moment forever. It seems like we were making love for hours. Time wasn't important and the only thing that matter is that we had time with each other.

We held each other in bed and she looked at me as I looked at her. I love you, she said. And I love you Michelle. We fell asleep in each other arms, and then Sheriff Judas came in the room. He told us to get dressed and meet Satan in his office. We got dressed as quickly as we could, and went into Satan's office. Satan stood by his balcony with his back facing us. He looks like he has something serious he wants to tell us. I am kind of worried because this is hell and there is nowhere to go if this goes bad.

Satan says, "Do you know what my greatest accomplishment was? For centuries people considered me a myth and something of a taboo created to scare people into following the path of God. But over time people started losing faith in God and so they turned to me. People will do anything and everything to get what they want out of life. People would sell their souls and the souls of their first born child to get a piece of happiness.

Unlike God I don't have to prove to people I exist. I exist because in each and every human there is a desire to be evil. God exist for the soul purpose of having people worship him because he created them, so they have to have the fear of God in them. People fear me because I am equal to no one, and God want people to believe that it is evil that destroys a person.

Evil doesn't destroy souls; it's the hopes that if you stay on the righteous path that good will prevail. So, my greatest accomplishment is letting Gods children hopes and dreams crumble to the point that they realize that God is the one that they shouldn't believe in.

But enough about me; I want you two to go to earth to collect the soul of John Baxter's first born child. When you get the child I want you to bring the child back to me. When you both prove yourselves to me you will be able to travel the world, be with high society, and more powerful than you both ever could of imagined. But I do have a few rules before you leave. You both are not allowed to come in contact with your love ones. If you disobey me the punishment will be worse than burning in hell.

If you reunite with a love one I will destroy them, and make you watch them burn in hell. Both of your families will be taken care of as long as you both stay away from them. Don't try to ask God for help, and try to escape from hell because I will hunt you both down myself. You both will have a dagger to carry with you. You don't really need a weapon with you powers, but it fun to torture your victims with it.

You will possess superior strength, be able to travel the world just by thinking of the place you want to go as you shimmer in and out from one destination to the next. You will be as fast as a cheetah and be able to sore the sky like an eagle. You will be as versatile as cat. You will be powerful, feared by all and have the world kneeling before you. All you both have to do is follow the rules and everything you every wanted will be yours."

Thinking to myself I have everything I have ever done in my life have come down to this moment. I tried to live a good life, and not do sinful things. I don't think I was one of the chosen ones on Gods list. I really don't care anymore; and this isn't the time to question why I here. I am in hell, and I am stuck here whether I want to be or not. It is time that I face the facts that God doesn't care about me, so I don't care about him.

Michelle say, "Honey just look on the bright side we are not suffering like the rest of the poor souls. The upside is that we will at least live well even though it comes at the expense of others. Besides, we have no choice but to follow his rules, or he will destroy our love ones. We have to follow the rules at least until we can find a way to get our love ones out of harm's way. I am just happy that I don't have to go through this ordeal alone. I love you so much Michael."

I love you too Michelle. We went back to our room, and sat there for a while thinking about our first assignment. Hell has no sense of time, so in earth years I haven't been on earth for about a year now. Time stands still in hell as Father Times moves on, so that earth can carry on without us. I don't know if I am ready to take someone's soul, and I don't think I am ready to suffer the consequences if I can't give him what he ask of me.

Michelle grabs my hand, "Michael come with me. When you look at the window what do you see?"

I feel like I am on top of the world. I feel like I am above everyone and everything.

Michelle smiles and says, "We you rather be sitting on top of the world, or burning in the bottom of hell's pit. I know I don't want to burn for an eternity in hell. I would rather do what he asks of us because God hasn't given us a way out. Believe me sweetie if there was another way, then I would have taken it. So if killing is what we have to do, then let's just do it!"

Chapter 7

It is 2011 Thanksgiving Day on earth and everyone seemed thankful for what they have. We arrive on earth dressed in all white. We looked like angels, but when they felt our presence they know that we are from hell. We look, and talk just like everyone else, but only certain people know who we are. The people that have sold their souls, sinners, and the psychopaths all know who we are. The people that are considered Gods children feel our presence, and try to avoid us all together.

Michelle and I are like Gods amongst these humans who look for God for help instead of doing things on their own. I could feel my spirit becoming corrupted by the evil presence inside of me, and I am afraid to say that part of me wants it to kill the good in me forever. I can't ever see my family, or love ones again.

The only love one I have is Michelle, so if evil is what I am destiny to become I welcome it with open arms.

We are in their house and they both are upstairs in the baby's room. I look around the room and I see pictures of his family looking so happy together. His wife is holding the baby in her arms as her husband stand beside her with a smile of a proud father. This place looked like a happy home. He made some bad choices and got involved in something he shouldn't have.

Maybe he didn't totally understand the consequences of his actions, but today he will realize that the reward isn't greater than his consequences. We have to do something that we don't want to do and that is breaking up a happy home. How do we do this, and what other choices do we have? I looked at Michelle, and she could tell that I didn't t want to go through with this. Michelle looks at me and says, "You know we have to do this; we don't have a choice."

They knew what the consequences of their actions were and they did it anyway. If anything we are doing that child a favor. I know I wouldn't want to grow up in a family that would sell my soul to the devil for materialistic and superficial happiness.

How desperate does a person have to be to give the soul up on their first born child because they can't make it on their own in the real world? So, let's just get this over with, so we can stop feeling guilty for what stupid mistakes these people have done. I know that she is right, but I can't help but feel that we would just make things worse for them by taking the only thing that most likely is keeping them from going to hell. Maybe their souls belong to hell already, or maybe they were too afraid to sell their own souls. I don't know why they chose their child as though it was a bargaining chip.

All I know is when someone commits a sin; it doesn't help by committing another sin as result of its actions. We shimmer into the room, and the mother is in the nursery sitting in the rocking chair breast feeding her one week old son. It was Thanksgiving, and they were having their first Thanksgiving alone as a family. Mr. Baxter was downstairs in his study Mrs. Baxter looks up, and looks at us standing in front of her. We are here for your son Mrs. Baxter, which has become sole possession of Satan due to the fact that Mr. Baxter upon request of a job on Wall Street, the rich life and to have a family of his own.

We held up our end of the bargain, so now we want the child. Michelle says to Mrs. Baxter, Don't make is harder than it has to be. You are able to have more children now thanks to Satan. I can't say I know what you are going through right now, but your husband made a deal with Satan. Your first born son is now the child of Satan.

So, if you will give us the child we will be on our way. The Mr. Baxter screams upstairs from downstairs, "Honey is everything ok up there?" Mrs. Baxter is holding on to her baby tight. She is coughing up blood and tears are falling down her eyes. Her makeup is running down her cheeks. She whispers to the baby, Mommy loves you, and I will never let you go!

Mr. Baxter runs into the run and looks at us. Hello Mr. Baxter we a look of disbelief. You knew this day would come someday. Mr. Baxter so don't look so surprised I told him. You didn't t think that Satan was going to give you a pass now did you? You had to think in the back of your mind that this day would come. Now if you give us the child you could get started on making a new family. I don't mean to sound insensitive, but you brought this on yourself. But, you know what the worst part is not letting your wife in on your dirty little secret. Now without Satan's help she wouldn't have this child today, or be able to bare children at all, but to sell the soul of the first born is cruel. If you were a real man Mr. Baxter would have sold your own soul and not the soul of your first born child?

You are nothing but a coward Mr. Baxter. You couldn't hold down a job. You couldn't get your wife pregnant. You can't even be a father to your child. We should be taking your soul, and not your child. Mr. Baxter cries out, and says, Please don't take our child away from us!

Please take myself instead. Please I will do anything you want, but please don't take our child away from us. I will sell my soul if that what it takes to keep my son here with his mother. They have nothing to do with this, so please take me! You know what Mr. Baxter that was a touching and moving speech. But I am going to have to say no to your request, so just give us the child. Michelle holds the father back as he tries to move towards his wife. I turn to his wife and reached for the child. She had a look on her face that only a mother with love in her heart could give.

The love that she possessed for her child was so powerful that it made me hesitate for a moment. Michelle pushed the guy on the floor and snatched the child out of the mother's arms. The mother started hitting Michelle with every fiber of her being. Mr. Baxter got up, and I grabbed him by his neck. I held him in the air, and told him to just let it be. I told him what's done is done. It was nothing that he could do to change what he has done. I put him down, and he gasped for air as he hit the floor. Mrs. Baxter kept on getting up as Michelle kept on knocking her down. I pulled out my Dagger and held it to her neck. I whispered in her ear that she had a chance to start over, so let this be a lesson to them not to put their trust in a God that doesn't value life instead destroys it. Michelle put the baby back in its crib and looked at me.

Even though we were ten times stronger than them the love that they had for their child was just as strong. We knew that it wouldn't be easy to get this child, but we didn't think that we would encounter this much of a fight.

They both came at us at full speed. Mr. Baxter came at Michelle and Mrs. Baxter came at me.

We both took out our daggers and as they approached us we drove the daggers in their hearts. They both tried to get up. They both started to grab at our pants legs as they bleed to death. They were dying, but they were fighting to the end for a child that they have only had a pleasure of being parents of for three days. It was their last Thanksgiving and the last time they will see their child. I didn't care if they went to heaven for dying for their child and asked their God for forgiveness.

But the soul of their child now belonged to Satan, so even in death they will be childless. We were dripping in blood from the first. Our white clothes were covered in red. Our hearts and souls were forever stained by their willingness to fight to the very end. They fought to the death.

Even though they were fighting a losing battle they still fought, and for that I feel they deserve to rest in peace. Michelle picked up the baby, and we shimmered out to where the portal was. I didn't notice before that we were in Los Angeles and I haven't been out of the city of Chicago since I was a little boy.

We didn't have time to take a tour of the city, so went through the portal and stopped for a while as we reached Limbo. Is this what our lives have come too? Are we becoming the people that we have despised? Michelle what are we doing here? Michelle looked at me with the baby in her arms and said, "We were forced into this world and we didn't ask for this.

Those people that sold their souls to get what they want out of life got what they deserved. We are good people, and good people always get the shit end of the stick. We lived good lives, and this is what we got in return. We didn't do anything wrong, so if anyone is to blame for what we are doing it would be the Lord up above. So, don't beat yourself up and now it is up to us to live for ourselves."

Michelle you are right let just go give Satan the child. The sooner we get him the child the sooner we could but this all behind us. I hope to God that this kid doesn't suffer. I mean I just don't want this kid to not end up like us. If it wasn't for his father the child would be safe at home, or wouldn't be born into a world that would sell his soul for personal gain. I can't understand what would make a person want to do sell their child soul, or even their own. There isn't enough money, materialistic things, or people in the world that would make me sell my soul. We went into hell, and arrived at Satan's castle.

This was the first time I really looked at it, and was the first time I stood speechless over the perfection of the architectural design of the building that was built like a castle. We went in, and there were people dressed up sitting in rooms as we walked by down the hallway to Satan's office. I opened the door, and Satan is on the balcony. Michelle with the baby in her arms walked in with me.

Satan with his back facing us tells us to come out onto the balcony. We walked over to the balcony, and there are over a billion souls outside looking up at us on the balcony. It was like we were royalty. It was like a special event or something. We didn't know what to expect from our new way of life. I was afraid that he would feed us to the crowd for showing compassion, or humiliate us to the point that no one feared us. I didn't know why it was more important to me now for us to be feared than it was to save the soul of this child.

Satan is looking out into the crowd and says, "My people today mark a dawning of a new era. For no longer will we be second to Heaven. We are to be feared and respected. It is our time to show their God that this is our universe to control. It is our time to show him that earth is

147

for us to conquer. It is our time to show him that Heaven is beneath us, and they should bow down, and beg for us to show mercy on them.

Here today I have two souls that were lost, but now have seen what my blessing will give them. They have a child for me of a man that sold his soul to get what he needed out of life. They took the child from them, and they brought him back to me. They understand what I can do for them, and no that there is no such thing as blessings from God. I AM GOD! AND TODAY YOUR GOD WILL GIVE YOU ALL A SOUL. FOLLOW ME, AND YOU WILL LIVE A POWERFUL LIFE. DISOBEY ME, AND YOU ALL WILL BURN FOREVER. FEAST ON THIS CHILD, AND ENJOY BECAUSE THERE ARE MANY MORE TO COME. EAT MY CHILDREN EAT!"

He grabbed the baby out of Michelle's arms and without any hesitation he threw the child over the balcony into the crowd. It was like a massacre out there. There were people killing one another like rabbits. There were people like dogs fighting over a bone. Blood was everywhere, and everyone was fighting as though that was their last meal.

Michelle closed her eyes and turned away a couple of times. I on the other hand whispered to myself dear God what have I done? Satan went into his office, and sat in his chair. We stood by his desk and looked at him. Satan looked at us and said, "You did good and for that you both will be greatly rewarded. You will be able to travel the world just by thinking of where you want to go. You will be able to go anywhere on earth and no one will be able to stop you. You will live the life of luxury, and be feared by all.

Your powers will intensify with each soul you take, and keep as your own. The good in you will die as you take the souls of your prey. It doesn't t matter if they are good or bad if they make a deal with you their souls belongs to you.

For now the souls you get are yours and you can make deals with whomever your desire.

But you are forbidden to make deals with God, angels, or people who sole purpose is to do well. You both have a second chance at life, and to live the lives you have only dreamed of. So, do as you are told, and you will live on top forever. I felt sick to my stomach as he congratulates us for a job well done. Michelle held my hand tight and I just smile as he blessed us.

We didn't want to be in his grace, but what choices did we have. As I walked through the valley of the shadow of death the only thing I feared was the person that I was becoming. I didn't t have the armor of the Lord to protect me from the evils of the world because I have now become the one thing I feared the most the child of Satan. We left his office, and went back in our room. Michelle looked at me, and said, I know this is not what you had envisioned when you thought you would become successful. I know that you thought that God would bless you with a glorious

of blessings on earth, but God has forgotten about us.

You are his forgotten son and I am his forgotten

daughter. We didn't have a chance to make our own

destiny because our destiny was forced on us. We was

given to hell, and put in the middle of their war. So, now it

is our time to live for us. For no longer shall we put our

faith in a Lord that has abandoned us. For no longer shall

we believe in a God that lives his child behind to get

slaughtered. We are now the children of Satan and our

destiny is for us to control. I know this will hard for us to

accept, but in time we will accept the fact that we can only

trust each other.

Michelle I know what you saying is true, but I can't

believe in someone evil. I am not saying that I will put my

faith in God. I am saying that the only one that you are the

only one other than my family that I can trust. I don't trust

God and I don t believe that being good will get you into

heaven. I believe that free will is a way of God not taking responsibility for the actions of his children. He sits back and watches his children mess up. There are so many people messing up and he sits back and does nothing. How can a God who is so powerful sit back and let his children suffer?

FREE WILL! FREE WILL IS NOTHING BUT FALSE HOPE FOR THE WEAK! IF THE INFERIOR BEINGS THINK THAT IT EXISTS, THEN THEY DESERVE TO PARISH!

We put so much faith in someone that we never seen. We put so much faith in someone that does nothing, but gets all the credit for the good things that happens to us. It's not a miracle when someone makes it out of surgery, or escape death. It is not a blessing from God when someone gets money to pay their bills, or achieves their goals. Everything that happens in our lives is because of what we do not because of divine intervention. Forget divine intervention. FORGET GOD!

Michelle starts crying and says, "Michael I know you feel that you have been betrayed by God, but we can't think about the past. We must move forward and concentrate on our future. We have to believe that we can overcome these obstacles that we are facing now and live our lives for ourselves. We don't have to be good or evil. For us there isn't a reason for us to choose and there isn't a place to call home.

We might work for Satan and we might have been a child of God, but we must now just live. We are not like anyone else and we don't have to follow anyone. We are at the top and there is no one that can take us down. We live for the moment and we exist to please no one."

Michelle we can't leave hell and if we do he will destroy over family. He has forced us to choose, and he knows that we will not risk destroying our family for our own happiness. We are not living for ourselves and we can't just live freely. We are restricted in some respects, so Satan is our leader now. I don't like being made a fool of. It seems as though God has discarded us and Satan picked us up out of the trash. So, don't sit up there and say that we are better off from before.

Michelle looks at me and for the first time she looked like I had taken her soul. We held each other close in deep thought as if every seconded counted. I wiped the tears from her cheeks and gave her a kiss. I kept apologizing and she held me close to her as if letting me go would separate us forever.

I didn't realize how strong the evil spirit inside of me was growing. Each day that I spent in hell I grown closer to the evil in me. I felt the power of the evil spirit and it had replaced the Holy Spirit me. I felt like a good person that was now trapped in a person that was damned. We were rewarded for destroying a happy home. I can't believe that our happiness has come at the expense of someone else's sorrow.

But that is now in the past, so I have to look toward the future. I don t know what the future has in store for Michelle and I but what I do know is that she is the only thing in hell that keeps me from embracing my evil side. My family kept me from selling my soul before I ended up in this mess.

A few weeks go by and Sheriff Judas comes to us. The Sheriff smiles and says, "You two have done well, but now it's time for your next assignment. Now you have a chance to take your souls to keep after this assignment. After this assignment you can enforce your own will on others, keep the souls for yourselves, but have legion to Satan. All you have to do is turn as many souls as you possible can against their God and make them put their faith in Satan and keep the tasty treats.

Your next assignment is the Jefferson family and you will have to take the soul of Mrs. Johnson and her unborn child. She has sold her soul to Satan for vanity, a husband and a luxurious lifestyle. She agreed when she was a grad student in medical school struggling to pay back her loans that she would do anything to be beautiful, married and wealthy. She agreed to sell her soul and her child for instant fame, a family and fortune.

She is now a world- renowned Surgeon, a model, has a husband that loves her and a child on the way. She has everything she asked for and now it's time for her to pay up. Take their souls and you will be free to persuade anyone you want to sell their souls for you both to keep."

It's now Christmas Eve and snow is falling from the sky. We teleported ourselves to New York in Upper Manhattan and children were building snow mans on their front lawns. Kids are running up and down the streets having snow ball fights. There are carolers singing to a family down the street. The neighborhood is filled with Christmas lights on the trees and houses.

There is love, happiness and the Christmas spirit in the air. I don t know whether to cry, or throw up. This is making me sick, so we both teleported into the living room of the Johnson's family home. The husband is not home and Mrs. Johnson is sitting in the kitchen with her cook. They are both laughing as the cook takes ginger bread man cookies out of the stove. We walked slowly into the kitchen as they both turned and looked at us.

They could feel our evil spirit approaching their kind hearted souls. The cook must have known somehow because she jumped in front of her boss. I pushed her to the floor and stepped on her neck. I told her to stay out of this and we might let her live. Michelle walked towards Mrs. Johnson and said, "You lived a good life Denise. Your time has come to an end. Because of your selfishness your unborn child will never see the light of day. Not only will

157

you have to die knowing that you sold your own soul, but you didn't even give your child a chance to live. You don't deserve to live and your soul now belongs to us."

Denise looked up at Michelle and me as she crawled into a corner of the kitchen. She bowed her head and said, "Lord give me strength for I need your guidance. Lord forgive me for what I have done and don't let my selfishness take the life of my unborn child. Please forgive me Lord and have mercy on their souls.

My Lord for they don't know what they do. Satan has taken control of their souls and they need your guidance Lord. In the father and the Holy Spirit I beg of you my Lord for your help."

With an evil smirk I look at her and said, "Save your prayers for someone who cares. Your God doesn't care about you or me. You can pray to him all you want, but the fact that still remains we are still taking your souls.

There will be no divine intervention here today, so accept that your Lord doesn't t care about you.

CALL OUT TO THE LORD MADAM, AND HE WILL ACCEPT YOU SEE IF HE WILL LET YOU INTO HEAVEN! CALL OUT TO THE LORD, AND HE WILL DELIVER YOU FROM SIN!

The cook screamed out. I grabbed Mrs. Johnson and held her up by her neck. I pushed her in a corner and whispered in her ear. Because of your disobedience the death of your cook Susan is on your hands. Michelle walked over to Denise and held her arms as I walked over to Susan who was crawling towards the living room. I pulled her by her hair back into the kitchen.

Mrs. Johnson screamed leave her alone it's me you want. I pulled out my dagger and picked Susan up off the floor. I held the dagger up to her neck and smiled. WHERE IS YOUR GOD NOW? I shouted your God can't save you, and then I slashed her throat with the dagger. Susan fell to the floor and Mrs. Johnson fell to the floor screaming NO, NO, NO oh God No! Blood covered the floor, and we were soaked in her remains. Her spirit had unfortunately gone to heaven, but her body was massacred by us I was thankful that at least she died in pain before she left earth. Now she can watch her boss friend from heaven die on earth. Let's take this soul and go back home.

We both held our hands around Mrs. Johnson's neck and then stabbed her with both of our daggers. Her blood flowed out her body like the River of Jordan. The spirit of the child went into Michelle and Mrs. Johnson's spirit went into me. I felt so alive. We felt like we were unstoppable and it was the best we ever felt in our lives.

Blood was all over us like we were being baptized in evil. I felt great, and didn't t care what I had to do because I wanted more. We walked out the house, and waited for the husband to return. The clock struck twelve and it's now Christmas Day. The husband walks up the stairs, and the door is open. He walks in and there is blood on the carpet in the front room.

He walks into the kitchen and finds his wife that carried his unburned child with the cook lying beside her both dead. He kneeled to the floor as he cried out to God NO, God NO! We came in and we told him the truth.

Michelle pushed him to the floor, and we laughed as we teleported out. The police came and arrested him. Mr. Johnson couldn't talk because he went into shock. He went to jail for the murder of his wife, unborn child and cook. He couldn't speak after his dramatic ordeal and went insane.

Mr. Johnson couldn't explain what had happened, and if anyone could have or who would believe him. We owned most of the world, and evil protects the sanctity of evil. I couldn't believe that I felt so alive, and I couldn't believe it was because of Satan. I didn't know whether to thank Satan, or spilt at him for making me feel this way. When I was on earth even God couldn't make me feel this way. I lived a good life and I stayed on the right path and I still got screwed.

My mother worked long hours without hardly any sleep for her family after my father died and we still suffered while the sinners prospered. Now because of my situation my family is taken care of and I was living an amazing life.

How has a righteous God left good people here to suffer while bad people prosper? So, I stopped caring about what God would think of me and if my family would approve of the decisions I made in this past year. Michelle and I didn't feel like going back home. So, Michelle and I went to Rome. We went to the Vatican because Michelle said she always wanted to go there even though we resented everything they stood for. We went to where the Pope was and it was heavily guarded.

We could feel the spirits of the saints, the good souls, and the heavenly spirit surrounding him. It wasn't a good feeling walking around the Vatican, but I wasn't

afraid of anything at this point. One of the Popes guards

came out and told us to leave. He told us that our kind

wasn't wanted there and that we should leave.

So, I grabbed the man by his neck and told him that

if he didn't leave us alone that I would send him to hell. A

voice from afar said, "Put him down! The voice was soft,

but it had power behind it. We looked down the hall and in

all his glory the Pope graced us with his presence.

Michelle smiled and said, "What have we done to

be honored with your presence. "SILENCE," said the Pope.

The Pope stood there with his staff and with his head held

high. I didn't feel as powerful as I did when we first

entered and neither did Michelle. He looked at Michelle

and said in a soft tone Leave us. She looked at me and said

whatever you have to say to him you can say to me. I will

be ok baby; I want to hear what he has to say.

Michelle said, "I will go for you; I will look around maybe there are some souls I can take back home." What do you want old man; I don t have all day to talk. The Pope stood there with his staff and smiled. The Pope said, "You are heading down a path of destruction and at the end there is nothing but despair. God hears you when you speak to him. You have to believe in his words because he believes in yours. God is listening, so it is now time for you to listen to him. The devil tells you want you want to hear and you will find out that God is the one that loves you.

Put your faith in God again and God will show you the way back home."

STOP, STOP, STOP WITH ALL THE BULLSHIT! I AM SICK AND TIRED OF HEARING THAT GOD LOVES ME. WHERE WAS GOD WHEN I WAS IN HELL? GOD LEFT ME IN HELL, AND THE DEVIL IS THE ONLY ONE THAT LET ME OUT! IF GOD CARED ABOUT ME, THEN I WOULDN'T BE IN THE SITUATION

THAT I AM IN! SO DONT TELL ME THAT GOD

CARES ABOUT ME. GOD DONT CARE ABOUT ME,

AND I DONT CARE ABOUT HIM! WHAT I CAN TELL

YOU ABOUT GOD IS THAT HE LET THE EVIL ONES

PROSPER, AND THE GOOD PEOPLE SUFFER. AND

YOU GOT SOME DAMN NERVE TALKING ABOUT

GOD WHEN YOUR PRIEST ARE MOLESTING LITTLE

BOYS IN THE CHURCH, SO DON T TELL ME THAT

GOD CARES. GOOD PEOPLE PRETEND NOT TO BE

EVIL AS THE EVIL PEOPLE STAY TRUE TO

THEMSELVES. YOU KNOW WHEN SOMEONE IS

EVIL, BUT YOU CANT TELL WHEN A GOOD

PERSON IS LYING. SO FORGET GOD, AND I CAN

CARE LESS ABOUT YOU!!!

I lost my cool, and a burst of energy came from my

hands. It was like a black gust of wind that went straight at

the Pope. It was pure evil trying to destroy the good in the

Pope. The Pope swung his staff and the dark light

disappeared. It didn't even make a dent on the Pope. The Pope stood there calm and he wasn't upset at all. I was horrified, so I ran out of the church. Let's go Michelle; I want to go!

Michelle said, "What's wrong baby? Slow down baby; tell me what's wrong." I don't know what happened to me Michelle, but some kind of evil force came out of me. This evil force inside of me went straight to the Pope with the intention of killing him. It was as though something inside of me wanted to destroy the Pope because he is one of the closest being to God on this earth. I don't know what is happening to me, but it seems like I am dying inside. I am scared Michelle, and I don't know what to do. Michelle looks at me, and grabs my hands. She looked into my eyes and says, "They are trying to scare you baby.

They don't care about us and we don't care about them. All we have other than our families are each other. I love you baby and I am only telling you the truth. I will never lie to you, so I am telling you now that God has turned his back on us. I am feeling so much pain, and I can't believe this is it for me. I can't believe I will never see my dad again. I can't believe God has left me behind. I am his forgotten son and he doesn't care about me. I can't see my family again and they don't know where I am. My family doesn't know if I am dead or alive.

My family is probably crying over me thinking that I am dead, and they will never know that God left me behind for the devil to take. Forget God I don't care anymore; I had enough. God left me behind, so in hell I am stuck. So, don't tell me that God cares about me. I forgot about him already and his so called divined plan for me. It feels like that my mind; body and soul are engulfed in flames.

Thanks to Jesus I will never be the same. Can you hear me now; I will never change. If you want to point finger you are the one to blame. I use to think that you were the man. You messed up my life; and you messed up my plans. If this is a test then stick an "F" across my chest.

My faith in you has been laid to rest. Don't ask me to pray for you to help me. I Forsake you, and your son because you no longer have any respect coming from me. As the tears fall from my eyes darkness is what I now call home. I denounce you God; forget about me; just leave me alone."

Michelle you're right. All we have is each other. I can't depend on anyone else, but you. God left me to die, so I can't trust him. If anyone comes to me again speaking his words, then that will be their last words. This is my life now, and no one can change it. I made my bed, and I they will suffer the consequences.

Chapter 8

We weren't ready to go back yet, so we went Europe to look for souls. We were searching for the misguided, confused, and lost souls. I wanted to take it out on someone else, and see someone else suffer for a while. I wanted to see people give up their souls for a little bit of happiness because in the end their new found happiness would have just been an illusion. I can see it in Michelle's eyes that she wanted the same thing, and that we would find our own happiness in someone else's misery. It might not happen today, or tomorrow, but when they least expect it we will come back for their souls.

We went to visit Julie Peterson's an ugly duckling who wanted to be liked by her boss who wasn't paying her any attention. Julie has low self - esteem and is the only one in her family that isn't married. She is the youngest out of four girls, and is the only one still living at home with mommy and daddy. All Julie currently has that is her own is her job. Mr. Brooks assignment who doesn't know she exist beyond the office environment. Mr. Brooks calls her Judy and flirts with other women in front of her. Julie has prayed to God on numerous occasions to be beautiful, but God doesn't do vanity, so Julie turned to us. She closes her eyes and whispered to herself I will do anything, and give up my life to win the love of Mr. Brooks. When Julie opened her eyes Michelle and I was standing there. Julie was scared, and backed away from us. Don't be afraid Julie I say we aren't here to hurt you. Julie we are here to help you.

We heard you call for help and we are here to make all your dreams come true. See God doesn't t answer calls like this, so we will be more than happy to accommodate your wishes in exchange for something you have that we want. Julie starts to move forward and says, "What could I possibly have that would be of any interest to the both of you. I am just a child of God, but you two are angels of God. What do I have that you could ever want?

I would give anything for him. Just name it and I will gladly give it. I love him with all my heart and if I have something you need it is yours. Please help me. Whatever you want take it, but please can you help me? Just tell me what it is and it's yours!"

For the record we are not angels. We are merely under the services of Satan, but doing freelance work if you could call it that. We are only own bosses and we aren't angel. Angels are pathetic losers worshipping a God that picks and chooses who and what constitutes as a reason to help someone like you in desperate need of his help. All we ask of you is that you give us your soul. After you give up your soul to us we will grant you your happiness and in return when we see fit we will come back for you. We will let you enjoy your happiness until it reaches a certain length of time and without warning we will take your soul.

See in the end we both win. Julie you will live a happy and fulfilling life with Mr. Brooks and we will have your soul in the end for that. Julie in a state of shock says," Let me get this straight if I sell my soul to you not the devil I will live a happy life with Mr. Brooks. Where will my soul go? Will my soul burn in hell? What happens to my body? Will I be able to say good-bye to my family? What will happen to me? How long will it be before I die?"

Michelle with an annoyed look on her face says, "Shut up! Look at yourself you are not even on the man's radar. He doesn't even know you exist. The only reason he even pays attention to you is because you are his assistant. We could give you fame, beauty and the man of your dreams exchange for your soul.

Now before you answer think about what you have now. You may have wanted you need, but can you actually say you have everything you want? When are you going to tell yourself you deserve everything you want? Everyone else just takes and takes. So, isn't it time that you take what is rightfully yours. You don't need your soul after you die.

You will be able to live a happy life and we will come for your soul in due time. Trust me we have plenty of souls to get before yours, so you will have plenty of time to live a happy life with Mr. Brooks. We are not setting any time limit on your happiness so don't worry. All you have to do is say that you give up your soul to us an exchange for beauty and the deal is sealed to the Keepers of Souls."

On the other hand, I said with a smirk you can have it all if you give up the soul of your first born child. Now if you give up the soul of your first born child you will be able to have other kids with Mr. Brooks. You still would have your happy life with Mr. Brooks, and live a great life with your second born child. Just think of the life you two would be able to have together if you do this. You both would be able to grow old together and watch your kids grow up.

But if you don't give up your soul, then none of this will ever happen. You would have Mr. Brooks and fame, but you would not have any kids before your time is up. The choice is yours, so what is it going to be Julie? Julie grabbed the both of our hands accepting her fate. To seal the deal she had to sign the form in blood, and speak the words of our agreement. It almost seemed too easy for her to give up something that she didn't know how important it would become in the future. She bowed her head and said, "I Julie give up the soul of my first born child to the Keeper of Souls. SO IT HAS BEEN SAID, SO IT SHALL BE DONE!!!"

I could feel her soul slipping away even though it was the soul of her first born child she was giving up. I could see the innocence in her fading away and being replaced by greed. She wasn't the same Julie that we saw when we first entered. Julie was now a child of Satan, and she wore the title proudly for she wasn't like the rest. Even though Julie was only our first soul that we searched for on our own she didn't think about the consequences of her actions.

All Julie thought about was getting with Mr. Brooks and not what would happen to her first born child. She didn't ask what would happen to her child, or where would the child go. I guess Julie had soul her soul a long time ago, but now she just made it official. I wasn't here to judge, so she will have to live with her decision.

I thought I would be happy tricking an innocent soul into selling their soul, or the soul of their first born child, but all I felt was guilt. We left Julie Peterson's house and went to Asia. Asia was breath taking, but we had come here to search for souls. Michelle had named us KOS, which was Keepers of Souls our new title. I didn't t really bother me what we were called as long as she was by my side. But we were getting a little bored because on the way to Asia we took over 100 souls.

We took the souls of the homeless, blue collar

works, single moms, single dads, cancer patients and

anyone holding on to a thread of hope. So, Michelle and I

decided to split up to see who could get the most souls. We

had twenty-four hours to collect as many souls as we could,

and meet back at the same spot from which we came.

Michelle went south, and I headed north. I was excited, and

worried at the same time. This was the first time that

Michelle and I were apart. I was worried that I wouldn't see

her again, and thought this was the end. Michelle smiled at

me and said she would see me in twenty- four hours. She

kissed me on the cheek and whispered I will get more souls

than you sweetie so try to keep up. She left and we both got

to work. I arrived in a town where I thought I could get a

lot of souls, but it looked like it was abandoned. It looked

as though no one lived there.

I saw a woman carrying groceries into her home

with three little kids holding onto to her dress. May I help you with those groceries Miss? She nodded her head yes, so I put the groceries on the table. Her house was a mess. There was no heat, a rundown stove and beds on the floor.

Her apartment looked like one big room. So, I said Miss what if I told you that I could make all your worries disappear what would you be willing to give up? What if I told you that I could have you in a big house, a fancy car, and socializing with the rich? She smile and said, "I will call you crazy." Thanks for helping me with my bags, but if you would excuse me I have to prepare dinner for my kids.

Anna I know what you are going through and I could help you. All you have to do is ask for my help, and I would help you. All I want in return is your soul. You kids are going to starve to death in a few weeks, and you will lose everything. All you have to do is give up your soul to me, and everything will change for you, and your kids. She started crying and said, Get out of my house! I don't know how you know my name. I don't know who put you up to this, but I am not in the mood to play games. Get out of my house! Leave me and my family alone you freak! Get out my house now!!! With a smile on my face I looked her in the eyes, and said I will go. But before I go I want to tell you a story if I could. Let me tell you this one story, and then I will leave you alone forever.

I knew if I told her a sad story that she would do whatever I asked of her. I asked her if she would just hear me out first. She nodded her head yes, so I started telling my story. There was a man who once believed in God, and believed that he would answer his prays when he called on him. Now the man never asked for much, and when he did it was to help others. The young man cared more about others than he cared about himself. The man got a called that would reunite him with a love one; it was a once in a life time opportunities.

The answers to the all the young man's questions were going to be answered from his love one. The young man was excited about having this opportunity and thanked God that he answered his prays. He had a chance to make all his dreams come true.

However, when the young man got his opportunity to reunite with his love one God screwed him in the end. See the young man never got a chance to reunite with his love one, but instead he was left behind to rot in hell. God turned his back on the young man, and caused him to become what he is today a guy who heart is filled with evil.

The guy wanted to believe that God made a mistake, or this was so kind of test, but after a certain amount of time had passed he knew that God had forsaken him. He realized in the end that God didn't love him, and now he didn't love God. So, if you are thinking that God will answer your prays you are sadly mistaken. You are crying at night hoping that the next day would be better than the day before. As your kids fight over the scraps of meat you bring home that you call dinner. You hope that somehow so way so money would come in.

Your job doesn't pay much and you are barely making enough to keep a roof over your family heads. Your prayers haven't been answered because God doesn't care about you. I will tell you the truth. I want your soul and for your soul you will get absolute happiness. I know that you want a nice job, a nice big house for your kids, a father for your kids, and not to have to worry about money for the rest of your life. I can give you everything you ever wanted, and in return all I want is your soul.

You won't need your soul when you are dead. God doesn't care about you, so what does it matter if your soul goes to me when you die. If you wait for God to answer your prayers you will be still waiting after you die, and you kids will suffer because of it. Your kids will end up on drugs, in abusive relationships, and selling their bodies to pay the bills.

Do you really want to pray and depend on a God that makes you fend for yourself? Come on just start living your life for yourself. If you don't care what happens to you, then at least do it for your kids. Do your kids really have to suffer for things beyond their control?

Don't you want a life of happiness for your kids? Don't you care what happens to your kids? You have more than yourself to think about, and time is running out. I will go, so pray to your God now. I assure you that he will help you eventually. I started walking out the door, and she cried out Wait, Wait; please wait! I smiled and then I turned around.

All you have to do is say that you give your soul up to me, and you have forsaken God. You have to hold my hand, and denounce the words of God. You have to believe in your words, and lose your faith in God. You have to want your happiness and not ask for forgiveness.

You must believe that the Lord up above isn't a righteous God and that I am your God. You have to pray to me and believe in my words and the words that you have to do whatever it takes to succeed. She got on her knees, and held my hands. She started crying and said. I give up my soul to you for a new house, a new car, a husband and a rich lifestyle. I want to not have to worry about money ever again. I don't want to work anymore. I want my kids to have a father and I want a husband. I want my kids never have to worry about poverty, or having to suffer like I have. I want it all and for it all I give you my soul.

What Anna didn't know that she would live half of her life and see her kids only in their teens before I took her soul. She would get hit by a drunk driver who she fired for spilling red wine on her Persian rug during one of her fancy dinner parties in her mansion. Anna would live a rich and fabulous lifestyle with her husband who's a doctor. Her kids are all making straight A's in school and are all in private school.

I didn't care if she had a change of heart, or if she wanted to repent for her sins. Anna's soul was mine, and not even God could save her now. No one gave me a chance to live a normal life, so if you sell your soul you will not get any pity from me.

Anna didn't stop to think about the consequences of her actions. No one really thinks about the consequences of their actions anymore, and that is why I don't feel sorry for taking some ones soul. If someone would give up their soul for personal gain, then they deserve whatever happens to them in the end. In the beginning they say it's for their kids, or it is so they could get on their feet.

People claim that if they get the help that they need that they would be happy, but in the end they realize that the happiness that they are given wasn't theirs to accept in the first place. So, do I care about what happens to Anna in the end; she can burn in hell with the rest of them! I am getting a little bored, so I stop into this night club, and I see this waitress crying next to the restroom.

There is a line to get in the club about three blocks long, but I just by pass the bouncers and walk straight in. I am like a God now on earth and what I want I get. There wasn't anything I couldn't get and there wasn't anyone on earth that can stop me. I walk to the back of the club next to the washroom were the waitress was sitting on the floor crying. Dry your eyes Pam everything will be ok. I am here now, and all your problems will go away if you just put your trust in me. All you have to do is make a deal with me, and you will have everything you ever wanted.

She looked up at me and said, "How do you know my name? Who are you and what do you want from me? If you think I am some kind of whore then you are mistaken. Whatever you are thinking about doing to me just forget it.

We are in a packed club and I will scream rape if you don't leave me alone you freak!"

Now Pam is that anyway to talk to a guy that can solve all your problems. You just got fired from your job here at the club. You will be evicted from your apartment within the week. Your boyfriend is beating on you and taking all your money to shoot up. Your family has turned their back on you and they think you are a lady of the night.

Now if I am forgetting something let me know. I held out my hand and picked her up off the floor and took her into the back room. Get out now; I told the suits that we're running the club who were sitting in the back doing absolutely nothing. I set in the boss's chair, and told her to have a seat in the chair across from me. Wipe your eyes Pam because you have nothing to worry about now.

You are too beautiful to be sitting here crying. Let me take all your troubles away. Let me help you help yourself. She wiped her eyes and said, "How can you help me? Are you an angel or something? Why would you want to help someone like me? I have nothing to give you. I am broke, homeless and I have no one. I am all alone and I have nothing to offer you. What can I possibly have that is of value to you?"

All I want from you my dear is your soul. All you have to do is give me your soul, and you will have everything you ever wanted. You could be loved by many, be rich, have your family back, and never feel the oppression of a man again. Give me your soul, and you will be on the top of the world and looking down on the looser who once looked down on you.

Now is your time to get back at the people that mistreated you. Now is the time for you to live for you, and for no one else. It is your time to shine, and all I ask of you is your soul. She wiped her nose and said, "You can have my soul, so tell me what I have to do? What do I have to do? Do I have to shake on it? Are you the devil or something? Take my soul, but give me what I want?"

Just like that I had another soul, but her soul was a pathetic one. I didn't feel a challenge like I did with the one before. Pam showed me how pathetic mankind really was, and how easily a person can get manipulated into wanting this that they don't really need. She could have prayed to God, she chose to answer my call. I don't really care about her sad pathetic life. She is another pathetic little insecure woman that will get what she deserves in the end.

Pam will become a successful criminal lawyer and will marry a senator on Capitol Hill. She will have two little girls, and her family will be in her life. Pam will have a great life for the next ten years, and then she will die because she put an innocent guy in prison because she made a deal with a judge, DA. Her husband who was the Senator of Texas wanted her to put her client behind bars.

The client she had was the only suspect in a murder trial that got a lot of media exposure around election time.

The judge, DA, and her husband the Senator were dropping in their polls, and need his conviction to win. So, Pam cut a deal with the DA, and got him life without parole instead of the death penalty. Evidence was hidden from the trial thanks to her destroying it. The client got stabbed to death during a riot, which was later proven to be orchestrated by the guards. The brother of the accuser shot her coming out of the night club I meet her in that day I saw her crying on the floor.

She will bleed to death, and I will be there to take her soul. No one will help her, and no one will care because she didn't care about no one but herself. She was never at home, and her husband cared about his career. Their kids will eventually turn into their parents and I will take their souls as well. Pam didn't mean anything to the world and the world didn't mean anything to her.

I saw Pam's fate and she deserved everything she got. I have about an hour left before I reunite with Michelle and I have taken over 200 souls in one day. A part of me feels like a God and the other part of me feel like a dying soul. One thing that was clear to me that I no longer cared about society anymore. I didn't care whether I was taking the soul of a good person, or the soul of a bad person. I couldn't tell the difference between good and evil anymore.

Everyone had their reason why they would let me take their soul, or the soul of a love one for what I could give them. They all thought the happiness that I could give them is the answers to all their prayers. They pray to me to end their suffering and pain. I am like God to these people on earth that I considered lost souls. If a person is willing to give me their souls without questioning my motives, or choosing God over me well they deserve to suffer a horrific fate.

This job was so easy; it was like taking candy from a baby. This was more than a job; it was a way of life for me. I can't say I was blessed, but I felt like I was finally finding out my purpose, and who I was meant to become. Maybe this wasn't the path of was supposed to take, but this was the road that I ended up on.

I have no signs, no guidance, or help along the way. The only other person I can count on is Michelle. Michelle is all I have left. I can't see my family, so Michelle is the only family I have left. I love my family, but right now they don't exist in my world. If I am going to survive I can't show any weakness. I didn't care much about a lot of things if it didn't have anything to do with Michelle and me. People in general started to make me sick, and I treated them as if they were beneath me. They were beneath me, and getting their souls was me doing them a favor. Humans take everything for granted, and pray to a God that watches as they suffer.

Chapter 9

It was about thirty minutes left before Michelle will shimmer back to this spot. I see someone shimmering in and it is not Michelle. It is an angel and he is dressed in all black. What do you want I asked him? Get out of here before I clip your wings. I will not warn you again.

The Angel looked at me and said, "On the outer surface you remind me of your Lord, but on the inside you remind me of the Lord up above. You can hide behind his words all you want, but we both know that deep down inside your soul is pure. You cannot lie about who you really are no matter what you want others to believe. Sooner or later they will see the truth, and you will have to choose the road you want to travel on."

Save your speech for the weak, and spare me the psychobabble Angel. I don't need you preaching to me, and I don't need your pathetic God. Your righteous God turned his back on me, and left me to burn in hell. I don't have to explain my action to you, or to him. This is my life to live, and I answer to no one.

God doesn't still love me? Don't tell me that God really is here for me, and has been there on along. The only thing that I have is Michelle, and the love for my family. God put me in the situation that I am in. I have ruined so many lives because of God, and I am seen the truth in people. I have finally realized that I hate the world, and I hate humanity.

When I get through with the world there will be nothing left for God to take. God has given people free - will, and the willingness to choose their own fate and destiny. You can tell your God that I will make sure that his people go to hell free of charge. The Angel walked over to me, and stared me in the eyes.

He looked me in the eyes and said, "My name is Christopher and I once felt the way that you felt. I know

that you think that God doesn't care about you, but he does.
I know that you think that you are all alone, and evil is the
able thing you can turn too. God hears you when you cry
and he feels your pain. Put your faith in the Lord Jesus
Christ and he will deliver you from sin.

God will take all your pain, and suffering away.
Come with me and God will take you home. Come home
Michael; come home! I grabbed the Angel by his neck, and
then Michelle shimmered in. What is going on; Michelle
shouted. I am just taking out the trash Michelle; I will be
with you in a minute. Sit back, and enjoy the show
Michelle. I am going to take the soul of this Angel, and see
what goes does for his precious Angel.

So, tell me Christopher is your God going to help
his pathetic little Angel out of this predicament, or am I
going to have to snap your neck just for the hell of it. I
don't hear you talking now Christopher. Where are your
words of wisdoms now Christopher? Does the devil have

your tongue Christopher? Michelle set there in awe of what I was doing. Michelle was in total shock of what was going on, and she was left speechless. I could feel the spirit of the Angel slipping out of him.

Angels and Demons can get their souls taken away from them while they are on earth. We are just like human, but we are higher up on the ladder with are Lords. We are like immortals to humans, but to those that are equal to us we are like humans. So, I was in a position to take the soul of this Angel, but the consequence could cause chaos. I didn't care I wanted to send God a message.

I don't want God's help, and by taking the soul of Christopher will show God I have turned my back on him forever. I held Christopher up high and Michelle pulled out her dagger. Michelle gave me her dagger and told me to take his soul.

I stabbed him in his left wing as I slashed the blade right down the middle of it and then I did the same to the right wing. I then ripped off one wing, and then the other wing. Daniel was bleeding from his sides, and repeating to himself; Have mercy on his soul Lord for he know not for what he has done. I threw Christopher to the ground. His blood is now on my hands, and his death was only a sign of what was to come.

My eyes felt like it was on fire, my soul felt as dark as a starless sky. My heart was beating as fast as it has ever beaten. I stepped on Daniels neck, and said may God have mercy on my soul. May God kiss my ass because I don t need his mercy. I picked up Daniel who could barely stand up, and I started to feel the dark energy build up in me, and then out of know where a bolt on lighten hit Michelle and I. Michelle, and I flew about 10 yards back.

We both got up and Christopher was gone. God had taken Christopher back to heaven. God has left the both of us behind again. But this time I didn't want to go back to heaven, and I didn't care what God thought about me. I had everything I wanted, and I didn't need what he had to give. I wasn't like those humans who believed in the words of God, and thought that praying to God would eventually bring them blessings.

I wished I could have taken Christopher's soul and taken something from God because he has taken so much from me. Michelle kissed me, and then said, "God has just proven to us that he doesn't care about us. God has just sent us a sign that he only cares about a chosen few. It is his way or no way at all. There is no so thing as free will. God just tried to destroy us because we were messing with one of his Angels."

We would have been doing Christopher a favor if we would have taken his soul because God doesn't deserve anything. We went back home to hell. We each went home with over two hundred souls a piece. No matter what we did everything we did came out equal. A part we were missing something, and didn't feel whole. Together we were complete, and there was a balance. I loved Michelle more than I loved myself, and I felt her in my heart. She was the only thing kept me going in hell because without her my soul would have burned in hell.

I can see the truth in Michelle eyes and I knew she felt the same way with me. Sheriff Judas came to us as we were approaching Satan s Kingdom and said he needed to talk with us. Judas said, "You both are doing a great job, but there is something that you both need to do before you can reach your true potential. You will have to change God, and get God to strike back. Satan is impressed with his people who aren't afraid to stand up against God, and defy him. If you both rebel against God, and you both will be in Satan s blessings. As a matter of fact you could even challenge him.

You both are strong enough to even take Satan down. You both are at the top, and all you both have to do now is take control of your destinies. Look Judas; may I call you Judas? I don't care about what you think. I know what you are trying to do, and we are not the same two souls that you tried to breakdown before. I hate you, and if you weren't Satan s right hand man I would kill you where you stand. Now get out of my face you weak pathetic soul. Judas face started to turn red and he balled up his fists.

Judas said, Now you listen here you little errand boy! I brought you down here, and you wouldn't be anything without me. You both are pieces of shit that I transformed into diamonds. I made you both, and I can break you both. So, don't make me mad! Michelle took out her dagger and stabbed Sheriff Judas in the back.

Sheriff Judas grabbed Michelle by her neck, and held her up against the wall in the palace garden. I pulled out my dagger and stabbed Sheriff Judas in the back over and over again. He fell to the ground and dropped Michelle. Michelle and I stumped him repeatedly and he started to bleed.

Then all of a sudden it was a rumbling soon, and a dark cloud surrounded his body. Sheriff Judas body started to swirl around in the air, and separate into two dark clouds. One cloud went into Michelle, and the other went into me. I felt like I could go into heaven, and take down God himself. I felt like I was untouchable, and I could see Michelle face that light up like she couldn't be stopped. I felt so a high that I didn't want to come down. I didn't want this high to end, and we both just wanted more.

Michelle and I went to see Satan in his office. We walked down the hall, and everyone was kneeling as we approached his office. Everyone was treating as like we were royalty, and it felt great. We were fear and respect by everyone. I didn't t feel like the weak person I once did on earth. The good person inside of me that screamed out loud that held me back before was just a whisper now trying to hang on for dear life. Satan told Michelle, and I to have a sit.

Satan sat beside us and said, "My children I am so proud of you both. I am proud to say that your training has made you both warriors and there isn't anything else I could teach you two. I like that you both tried to take the soul of heaven's angels. And for you both to challenge Sheriff Judas who could have snap your necks without even blinking is truly amazing.

However, that wasn't Sheriff Judas. The demon that you destroyed is a shape shifter. He has the ability to change to anyone and anything he wants to. Chameleon was one of my top soldiers and one of my strongest fighters. If you had faced Sheriff Judas believe me you would still be fighting him as we speak.

Sheriff Judas has been there with me since the beginning and it would take a lot more than you two to defeat him. None the less what you did was a victory. I am proud of the both of you and for this accomplishment I am giving the both of you something really special.

That is why I am giving you both the power of Gods and now no one would be able to stop the both of you. It would take an army to stop my favorite soldiers now. People will look at you two with respect, and no one will be superior to either of you except me. Enjoy your gifts and your new found freedom. I said thank you to Satan and then we started to walk out.

Satan told Michelle that he needed to talk to her alone. He told me to go ahead, and that he wouldn't keep her long. Michelle look at me, and said I will be little while sweetie. So, I walked back to my room wondering why he wanted to talk to her without me. Everything we have done up to now have been together, and when he talked to us it was together. I hope that he isn't trying to have sex with the love of my life.

WHAT DOES HE WANT WITH MICHELLE? I DONT BELIEVE THIS IS HAPPENING TO ME! I HAVE TO DO SOMETHING!

I am sitting in our room alone waiting for her to come back. I am pacing back, and forth. It felt like an eternal that Michelle was gone. The longest time we were apart was when we were seeing who could get the most souls. I trust Michelle, but I don't trust Satan. I know that Satan is the emperor of darkness, so I can expect the worst. I can't tell him to leave her alone, and I can't stop him from having his way with her.

But if I find out he's touched her I will try my best to raise hell while I am down here. Michelle walked into the room and she looked fine. Michelle, Michelle is everything ok? She sat on the bed and gave me a hug. She said that she was ok, and there wasn't anything to worry about. I didn't know whether to question her answer, and just trust her. She didn't t have any reason to lie, but if Satan told her to lie then she had to be scared to tell the truth.

She started to kiss me. She whispered in my ear, "Take me Michael; take me I am yours! I started kissing Michelle and I ripped off her clothes and threw her on the bed. I started kissing her over and over. I sucked on her neck. I started to bite on her nipples, and pulling at them with my teeth. Michelle started screaming Oh Yes, Yes and Yes! She kept screaming it over and over. I worked my way down, started sucking on her sweet nectar. I started biting her, and pulling on her succulent peach with my lips. I started sucking and licking it. I sucked on her toes, and did the beast with two backs. I filled passion and no regret she started screaming my name. I turned her back over, and pulled her legs over my head. I ravished her mind, body and demonic soul until there was nothing left.

Michelle started pulling away and pushed me down on the bed. She got on top of me, and started riding me. Michelle started grinding on top of me. She kept shaking her head back and forth. She started rubbing on her breast and sticking her tongue out trying to lick them. The bed was shaking and squeaking. It felt like everything in our lives has changed us forever.

We went from making love to just having sex. We went from a level of intimacy that connected our souls as one to rough sex. The way we talked and the way we acted wasn't our former selves. We have now become a shadow of our former selves. I didn't really care because all that caring would do is make us realize that resolving it is hopeless.

So, we accepted who we had become, and knew that this is the way that it had to be. We stayed in hell for a while, and we were treated like royalty. Satan came to us, and told us that it was time for us to go back to earth to reap the benefits of high society. He came to our room, and we were shocked. We had never seen Satan out of his office.

Michelle and I stayed close to each other under the covers naked. Satan sat at the bottom of the bed, and said, "You two are like my kids and I want you both to have it all. I want you both to go back to earth to rule over high society. It is time that high society sees the true nature of evil. I want you both to put fear back into the world and show them who really has earth by its balls.

This is not a direct order, but a chance for you two to build your own following. You two have potential to become my prince and princess of hell. When you both go back to earth you will have fancy cars, live in a mansion, have private jets, and be rich beyond your wildest dreams. You two will never have to lift a finger again.

Everyone on earth will fear the both of you and never want to cross your paths. No one will be able to say no to you. Everyone will hang on your ever word and you will be able to crush the lives of those that tries to rebel against you both. You will be able to destroy the dreams of business that are trying to make a difference, but need money. You will be able to destroy the homes of families that have been on the land for years to build luxury homes. You will be able to walk passed good people and seen chills down their spines. Good people will tremble at your feet and change their path because you told them to. This is what the two of you are destined to do, so don't disappointment." Before we could say anything he was gone.

Michelle and I went to sleep and I started to dream about my past. This is the first time I was able to drift way. I didn't think I could dream in hell without it being a nightmare. But I was able to dream, but as faith would have it I was reliving all everything I buried in my past.

"Michael couldn't you have stopped him? Why didn't you save me? Michael why did you leave me? Where are you Michael? I need you Michael," is what

Andrew shouted from a distance. I tried to run as fast as I could to get to him, but I couldn't reach him.

He was covered in blood, and holding a knife in his hand. The closer I got the further he got. I felt so helpless. Andrew hang on little buddy I will protect you. I will save you. I am so sorry for leaving you. Don't move little buddy. Stay where you are Andrew. The wind started to blow, and I couldn't see a thing. I fell to the ground, and when I got up he was standing in front of me.

I gave Andrew a hug, and we stood there for a moment. Drop the knife Andrew. I am here for you little buddy, so you will never have to worry about anyone ever harming you again. Andrew smiled at me. I looked down at Andrew's hand, and I felt a sharp pain in my stomach. He had stabbed me with the knife that he had in his hand. Why are you doing this Andrew? I am here to protect you, and be there for you.

Andrew laid me on the floor, and put the knife in my hand. Andrew barely ever spoke, but he said in a whisper, "You have saved me many times, so now it is my time to save you. We don't have that much time. Just let go, and you will not have to suffer anymore. If you fight to stay alive, then I will not be able to save you from what is to come. Let go Michael, and you will be saved. Stay and you will have to suffer for an eternity." I reached out to Andrew as he walked away. Don't go Andrew! Don't go!

I woke up in a cold sweat. Michelle turned and looks at me. Michelle said, "What's wrong baby? Did you have a bad dream? Who is Andrew, and why was he trying to leave you? I know this is a lot to deal with, but I believe that if we stick together we will do fine. Don't worry about what Satan said. We have to do what is best for us and everything else will just fall into place. I love you and you love me. The only thing in this whole entire universe that matters is what we have right here."

Why did I have a dream about Andrew? My mind is racing. As I think to myself Michelle is laying in my arms clueless to what is going on. Was my past finally catching up with me even though I was in hell? What did Andrew mean by he was trying to save me? What did I needed saving from? Whatever was awaiting me I feel sorry for the person that thinks that they can challenge me? My little buddy was my friend, but he was the weak one not me. At that moment I felt like everything was really going to work itself out for the best.

So, now you want me to feel guilty for my past sins? Are you joking, or trying to test my faith? Whatever you are doing up there you can stop it with the tricks. I have given up on you a long time ago, so save your spiritual journey for some other poor sap. It has now been 3 years since I have accepted my life as a member of hell. I didn't have a choice like most of these souls down here, but God gave me no other choice.

We are now on earth and it's the year 2009 and we are in Hollywood. We are in the city where nothing is as it seems. We started walking down the street, and a limousine pulls up to us. The limousine driver steps out and says, "This is your limo Sir and Madam." We get in the limo and he drivers us to Beverly Hills where there was a mansion that stretch three blocks long. The gate of the mansion had M & M on it. The gate opened up as the car pulled up the drive way. The limo driver parked in the drive way and then opened the door for us.

We got out and the door was open. We walked in the house and it was amazing. The ceiling is about fifteen feet high. Michelle started jumping up and down screaming out loud; I can't believe this is all ours! We were the wealthiest couple in the world, and we are untouchable. I couldn't believe that we were living the good life, and it all came from the man downstairs. We didn't t have to stay on the straight, and narrow. All Michelle and I had to do was to be ourselves.

Michelle turned to me and said, "Baby we have our own limo driver. We have our own maids. It's all furnished, and it's all ours. Look sweetie on the table, its papers that give us ownership over 20 major corporations in the city. We own at least three fortune five hundred companies. We can do whatever we want sweetie and we can crush the lives of the people that took years to build their business."

Let's destroy their lives later Michelle, but for now let's go out dancing. The butler comes into the room and says, "Sir you both own over 10 night clubs in the city and the best one is called Club Hell on Saint Blvd. If I may speak frankly it's the best club in the world and it will be an experience that people of your caliber can really sink your teeth into if you catch my thrift." Madam this will definitely be an experience I can say you will never forgot."

Michelle and I got dressed up to check out Club Hell for ourselves. The limo driver came to pick us up, and drove us to the club. On our way to the club Michelle started kissing me and unzipped my pants. Michelle started putting her succulent lips on my manhood. Then moments later she got on top of me and I could felt my manhood inside of her. As she looked into my eyes I felt like everything in the world stopped. I started kissing her lips, neck and breast as she moaned out my name. Thirty minutes later we both climaxed and we were parked in front of the club. The driver yelled we are here Sir and Madam.

The line to get in the club was about 5 blocks long. There were people of all nationalities, gender, creed, sexual orientation, religions, and social class all trying to get into this club. The bouncers pulled the ropes back and we walked straight in. We were the power couple and I felt like a God. I didn't enjoy going to clubs before, and I felt out of place when I was there. I was a popular kid, but felt like certain places weren't for me.

If someone looked at me funny, then I would probably want to break ever bone in their body. Talking to women was easy, but finding the right one was a challenge. Michelle and I may never have crossed path if it wasn't for this unusual circumstances. I guess I can thank God for turning his back on me. It's funny how things work itself out.

If it wasn't for God I probably would have still been that pathetic loser. Hoping that someone would give me an opportunity to succeed in life was naïve of me to think that way.

We arrived at the club and the manager approaches us and says, "Let me be the first to welcome you both to your club. We are honored that you both has blessed us with your presence. Whatever you want and need here tonight please don't hesitate to ask. My employees are at your disposable tonight. Let me show you both to your VIP ROOM and let me just say that I am honored to be working under the both of your leadership."

We walked to the VIP ROOM and we sat down. The waiter and waitress were walking around with red wine. We were the only ones in VIP and there were over a hundred people behind a rope outside in line waiting for our approval to mingle with us in VIP. We were in control of who we wanted around us and I got to say it felt really good.

No longer did I have to pretend to like people that I hated. I didn't have to socialize with someone that made me sick. If I didn't like someone I could kick them out, or if I felt like it snap their necks. Michelle and I ran this town and no were strong enough to stop us. The first ones to come into the room and they were a couple. The couple had on what it looked like second hand stores dress clothes. The lady and guy both kneel by our feet. We sat in our own thrown. We were living like Gods on earth and this was just the beginning.

The couple kissed our shoes. The guy said, "Please let us be one of your followers and let us be in your company here tonight. We will forever be in your graces. We will worship the ground that you both walk on, so please grant us this request."

The guy's lady friend said, "Please my Queen let us stay in here and we will do whatever you ask of us. We will do whatever it takes to make you happy and we will not question you at all. We are willing to sell our souls to be in your good graces. We will do anything, so please let us stay!"

Michelle stood up and grabbed the lady by her neck. Michelle held her up in the air and said to her, "Silence! Did anyone ask you to speak? You do not speak unless you are told to do everyone here understand me? The only lady that is allowed to talk in this room unless told to is me. I should kill you where you stand you worthless peasants.

Now what I want you both to do is prove that you are worthy of being in our presence. As of now all we see are two pathetic souls trying to disguise themselves as high class. You both are two worthless middle class bottom feeders trying to hang with the big dogs. If I wasn't in a good mood you two probably would be swimming in a pool of blood right now."

Now, Now, Michelle let's give these lower class people a chance to prove themselves. What I want the both of you to do is go get the gun that you have under your seat in your car and shoot Father Johnsons at the local church a couple blocks down. Now if you both do that we will make sure that you serve no jail time and you will be in our good graces. Now if you disobey us you will never set foot in this club again. You both would go back to your middle class status and never associate with the high class ever again. I will make sure that the both of you burn in hell for disobeying us.

So, the couple left as they were told and we moved on to the next group of people. We let over forty people in and we let the ones that had sold not only their business, but their souls to us in. There were lawyers, doctors, scientist, nuns, preachers, priest, teachers, politicians, entertainers, athletes and many more.

Somehow a nun came in and stood before us covered in blood. She had a dagger with an angel engraved on it. Was she an angel in disguise? Did heaven send someone to kill us? Everyone stood still and all eyes were on us. Michelle stood up and said, "You can't stop us, so you should join us. We are not the enemy we are here to show the world that we are superior beings and that we follow no one. Put the weapon down and join us."

The woman pointed the dagger at me and says, "Your time on earth will end soon enough. I am not strong enough to stop the both of you, but in time you both will destroy all that you have. You all don't belong here and you all will pay for this with very souls. God knows and sees all. God knows and see all. The people stand by rushed her and tried to grab

There was one person left that wanted to come in, and it was a Saint. I didn't know which saint it was because I didn't care that it was. The Saint stood there and said nothing to us. Michelle shouted, "Get out of here; Leave us! Your kinds are not welcome here, so get out before we put you down!"

Michelle and I stood up, and our followers in the room surrounded him. The saint dressed in all black said, 'You both can fool people by hiding behind the shadows of your former selves. You both are using your pain to justify your actions. You know that God is here for you, but yet you still go in the other direction. You know that God hears your call, so it is time for you to listen. You both must listen to his words and he will set you free.

Tell the devil to get behind thy, so the love of Jesus Christ could move you forward. Believe in Christ because he has always believed in the both of you. Come with me, and I promise you that your sins will be forgiven. We are running out of time we must go now!"

Nice speech Saint Peter, but here is what we are going to do. I am going to take your soul and you are going to go to hell. The nun might have gotten away, but you not going to be so lucky. I thought your God would have been smarter than that to send another one of his people to me. You have some nerve setting foot in here, but I guess when you are a good person you always think that God will come to the rescue. God isn't going to save you now.

I pulled out my dagger and I stabbed Saint Peter in his heart. I put my hands over his heart. But before I could take his soul something happened to me. I fell back and I started getting dizzy. So, Michelle picked up the knife as the Saint sat in a pool of blood. She screamed at the followers, Get out! Get the hell out! Michelle stabbed Saint Peter in the heart over and over. She put my hand on his chest with hers and his soul split in half. His spirit went into the both of us as we sat there in a pool of blood. We had crossed the line and went into forbidden territory. There was no turning back, and we have sealed our fate. If there was a chance for us to get back into heaven, then we have just closed the door on that chance.

We were just seating there and the couple that we sent out early came back. Our guards were guarding the door. We got up off the floor and they handed us some new clothes. About twenty minutes later we came back out of our room and told the guards to let the couple in. Michelle and I sat on our thrown and the couple entered. The couple entered with the head of Father Johnson. The couple was covered in blood. The guy had the gun in his head, and his lady friend had the head in her hand. They both were horrified and we could see in it their eyes that they knew that there was no turning back.

Michelle got up and walked to the lady, and gave her a hug. Michelle smiled and said, "Sara I am proud of you. We are proud of you both. You both went out there and did what you were told no questions ask. You both didn't hesitate, or thought about the consequences of your actions. Now you both are one of us and you don't have to worry about hoping things will go right for you. No longer will you have to pray for a miracle because you will be able to create your own miracle. You both will be unstoppable and no one will be able to touch the both of you."

I told William to come to me, so I could shake his hand. I was proud of the both of them, they had earned our respect. Don't worry about the law, or even going to jail. You both are safe as long as you do as you are told. If you follow our guidance you will not have to worry about suffering like the rest of society. If you look at today s society you see people struggling to survive with a God that uses free - will as his escape goat for why they are in poverty. The God above believes that you have to pray to him, and he will bless you in return. Instead of God blessing people who pray to him every day, and night he get their hopes up. Nothing comes from praying as you both saw tonight. If God cared about prayer, or his people then he would have stop you from killing Father Johnson. God would have stopped us from killing one of his Saints. God only cares about himself, so the both of you should only worry about yourselves. You will worship us, but only to further your own personal gain. If you learn anything it is to not trust anyone not even the ones you love.

Michelle looked at me and said, "Sara and William that is all for now, so go up to the penthouse suite at the Eternal Life Hotel on Melrose. They left and Michelle was looking at me like I just betrayed her. I knew at this moment that maybe I should have kept my true feeling to myself.

Michael you can't even trust the ones you love? Are you insinuating that you can't trust me? What are you trying to say Michael? Michael what are you trying to say!!!" I am not trying to say anything Michelle let's just leave it at that.

Why do you want to know what I am trying to say? DO YOU REALLY WANT TO KNOW WHAT I AM TRYING TO SAY MICHELLE? I AM TRYING TO SAY THAT YOU ARE KEEPING SOMETHING FROM ME YOU LYING LITTLE WITCH! OH YOU THINK I DONT KNOW WHAT IS GOING ON BETWEEN YOU, AND SATAN. YOU WENT IN HIS OFFICE AND DIDN'T COME OUT FOR HOURS. EVER SINCE THEN WHEN WE GO BACK HOME YOU STOP TO SEE HIM ALONE, AND YOU ARE WONDER WHAT I AM

TRYING TO SAY. I SHOULD SLAP YOU FOR
PRETENDING AS THOUGH YOU DON'T KNOW
WHAT IS GOING ON!

Michelle stood up and looked into my eyes with
tears running down her cheeks and said,
"Don't think that you can get away with slapping me you
sorry excuse for a man. Well what are you waiting for slap
me! You are not a man Michael; you are an inferior
creature. If it wasn't for me you would still be rotting in the
cell. You are nothing to me and I regret every having you
inside of me. You are not a man and you are a poor excuse
for a human being. You can help mankind by ending your
own life. Please leave you disgust me"

I don't know what came over me, but all of a
sudden I grabbed Michelle by her neck. I tried to choke the
life out of her. I couldn't believe that I was doing this to the
woman that I loved and the only woman that ever truly

loved me. I could feel her life fading away and a part of me slipping away.

WHAT WAS I DOING? THERE HAS TO BE A BETTER WAY! LOOK WHAT YOU ARE MAKING ME DO! I threw Michelle against the wall. She left a crack in the wall, and she laid there crying on the floor. A few minutes go by, and Michelle looked up at me laughing. WHY ARE YOU LAUGHING? WHAT IS SO FUNNY? TELL ME WHY ARE YOU LAUGHING MICHELLE? WHY ARE YOU LAUGHING AT ME? TELL WHY YOU ARE LAUGHING, OR I WILL KILL YOU!

Michelle as she wiped the blood from her lips sat on the bed, and reached out for my hand. Michelle looked into my eyes and said, "You passed the test sweetie that Satan has special plans for you. Satan thought that you were becoming weak. He noticed that you were hesitating on getting soul and we both felt it in your heart that you are still holding onto the love for others. Satan and I kept on meeting to evaluate your progression. We were worried that you would let love get in the way of your destiny. You are a very powerful and respected man Michael.

The love that we have for each other shouldn't stop you from dominating, and conquering others. You have to be fearless, and do whatever it takes to get to strike fear in those beneath you. I would do whatever it takes to get to stay on the winning side, and that includes going against you. I would expect you to do whatever it took to get to stay in power if that also included going against me. I love you Michael but love is just another form of weakness that God gave us to be inferior to him.

I don't regret what I have done at all and I love the new me. I understand now, but if you think that I am slipping just tell me. I might have hesitated a few times, but that will never happen again. I hugged Michelle close to my chest and whispered in her ear: I love you baby, but if you ever do something like that again I will not hesitate to kill you where you stand, and that my dear is a promise. Michelle went to bed and I stayed up thinking about what went on today. I couldn't see and I didn't know what to think anymore.

Everything that I held dear to my life was now being destroyed. Even the woman that I love was trying to make me choose between her, and my new found power. I didn't think that I would ever have to choose power or love. I love Michelle so much, but love in hell doesn't really exist. There is no room for love down here, and now I am seeing that there isn't enough room for love in my heart. How can I accept not loving Michelle? Could I possibly ever accept not loving my family? I can accept this new way of thinking; I just can't accept what they are asking of me. I couldn't sleep so I went back to earth and I went to Chicago.

Chapter 10

I had to see my family even though I know it is forbidden. I didn't know where they were, but I could feel them. I used the love I had left for them to track them down. The closer I got to them the stronger the feeling inside grew. I didn't like what I was feeling, but I had to see them one last time. I had to see them before I gave up on love forever. The pains in my heart lead me to Highwood Park. My family was living in a mansion. I could see my mother as I looked through the window; she was playing with her grandchild. She was chasing little Jasmine around in the living room and my sister was sitting in the chair laughing at Jasmine. My family was happy and I was happy for them. I started to cry because I knew the rules, and if I broke them I will be the reason they die. I still love them, and even though it's been years since I last saw them my love for them has never changed.

It is the year 2012 and there is a new mayor of Chicago. Barack Obama and Joe Biden are our President and Vice President of the United States. The people that are truly happy in this world are happy because they were willing to do whatever it took to survive. God's will have no part in the world's success, he only exists in fairytales. The world has put God on a pedestal for too long, but that will change now that I am here.

Michelle and I will make Satan proud of us when we bring the good people in society down to their knees. I love my family, and I will make sure that they don't get caught in the cross fire. I will also make sure that Michelle's family is taken care of, but the rest of the world will suffer. The love that I have in my heart is only for people I deemed fit to live, so everyone else could just burn in hell. My family won the lottery and because of me they can live the good life. If I was still with them everyone would still be struggling to survive. No one helped us and we were barely making enough to survive.

We all prayed to God every night and day and nothing ever happened. God left me to die in hell, and now my family is financially stable. I thought God was supposed to help me not Satan. He has been there for me, and God is nonexistence. If you can hear me God do me a favor, and stay out of my life. Dad if you are listening I am truly sorry. I hope you can forgive me Dad for all that I have done.

Sometimes I wished I would have gone back to save the innocent souls trapped in hell. With all the power that I had I didn't have any remorse or thoughts of saving them until now. I could easily save them now, but why risk what I have for them? Maybe one day I will stop by their and see who is alive, so I can torture them. I can't afford to show anyone any kindness. If Satan or Michelle thought I had gone soft, then they would think I was unworthy of my power.

My life is now set in stone and there is no turning back for me. Everything I ever wanted will come from me destroying the souls of others. I will step on anyone in my path to obtain even more power than I already have. I have to be feared to be respected. I have to be ruthless to be admired. I have to be perfect to be superior those inferior to me. I have to embrace my full potential, so I can fulfill my destiny. I can't let love stand in my way because those that care for others are weak.

Those that are weak can't survive on their own, so they need someone to rule over them. I can't believe I left hell. I am here alone and I left without Michelle. I am my own person so I can do whatever I want. If they come looking for me I will destroy them all if they question what I am doing. I can do whatever I want and there is no one that can stop me. Satan can't even stop me. I am not afraid to die, or even burn in hell. Because to my family I am already dead and to the world I don't exist anymore.

The new Michael exists in a world that fears him, and he doesn't socialize with people that he can't benefit from using. I now believe that the rich and power needs to stick together. I also believe that the weak and the poor need to be exterminated. I don't know when I will return to hell, but I don't know if I am ready to leave my family. It has been about 3 years since I have seen them and they probably think that I am dead. The police gave up on the search for me after a month because Satan made them.

My family went on the news for me for years trying to find me, and to find out if I was still alive. There were people that reported to the media and my family that they saw me in cities around the world, but I was too powerful to be noticed by people in the lower class. I was kept a secret because that is what Satan wanted. My family has never given up, but with media turning their backs on them during their time of need made them stop searching. I don't

blame my Mom for giving up searching because as the

years went on it was killing her inside. I wish I would have

known this before, but I guess my soul was consumed with

power that it didn't see the truth right in front of my eyes.

Mom I am truly sorry and I love you all so much. Don't

worry about me I will be fine. Please forgive me and I will

always be here for you all. I love you all.

Everything felt out of place, and it was happening

so fast. I felt that I needed to makes things right. I didn't

like the person I had become. If I was going to be a

powerful being, then I was going to put it to good use. For

no long will I stand by and let anyone else down. It was

time to take a stand. People can stand for something, or

stand by while everything around them crumbles. I must go

back and save the people that was depending on me. I have

to go back.

Michelle is all alone in hell. I have to go back now.

If Satan find out where I am, and what I have done

everything I love will be destroyed. She can't fight him by

herself. I should have brought her with me. We could have

stayed on earth together, and let them come after us. I can

only imagine what is going on in hell right now.

Michelle

Satan comes in our room and says, "Where is Michael? WHERE IS MICHAEL? I jumped up. I quickly covered my naked body. He brushed my hair back with his fingers, and then he grabbed me by my throat. I can't breathe, and I am trying to push him away. I can't get away he is too strong.

The hold Satan has on me feels like it's going to crush the life I had left out of me. He looks at me, and says, "GO FIND HIM NOW!!! You can't do a simple job. Why do I bother with pathetic creatures like you? I should have left you where you were. Maybe you would be better suited as a child of the human's pathetic God."

He couldn't have gone far; he probably went back to the mansion. I will go find him; don't worry my Lord I will find him. Michael and I love it here. We have everything we could possibly want and more. Don't worry he will be coming through that door any minute.

Satan smiled and grabbed my arm and says, "I know where he's at and so do you. Bring Michael back, or you don't have to worry about coming back. I will make sure that my men hunt the both of you down and kill you both. Don't think that you can run from me because I am everywhere. I will find the both of you, and no matter where you go I will be there. I will never stop until I get you both back because I own you both.

Don't forget who gave you all of this and don't forget who you are. You are a part of me and you will never be able to change who you are. It is time for you to make him finish his transformation; he must embrace his evil spirit completely. You know what you have to do, so go do it. Now go find him, or you will find yourself burning in hell."

I started to walk down the street and I could feel someone behind me. I turned around and I saw Michelle walking towards me. Seeing Michelle now feels different and I knew that she didn't come to give me a hug. I knew that when Michelle was slowly approaching me that something was wrong. I didn't know what was going to happen, but I felt sadness in her heart. I felt pain and suffering in her heart.

As Michelle got closer to me her pain grew stronger. Michelle and I were face to face. She had tears running down her face. I wiped her tears off her face. She kissed me on the cheek and said that she was sorry for everything. I didn't know what she was talking about. She was starting to scare me and I was starting to freak out. What do you mean? What in the hell are you talking about? Let's go back home to our mansion and talk. Michelle, said, "We can't go back home Michael." Well let's go back to hell then Michelle. Can we go back to hell? Tell me what is going on Michelle you are scaring

me!

Michelle, started crying and said, "I never planned

on this happening. I was never meant to fall in love with. I

was just supposed to turn you evil and you were then

supposed to go on to be one of Satan's foot soldiers. But

something happened Satan saw something in you, and told

me to stay with you a little bit longer. He saw you as a

challenge, and he knew that you would be hard to break. I

didn't t think that I could ever fall in love, but with you I

did. You got to me and you made me love again.

Michael I am not who you think I am and I don't

have that much time to explain. I am Satan's daughter.

Satan and my mother who's an Angel in heaven met on

earth. Satan fell in love with my mother and then killed her.

Satan took me to hell and after he killed my mother. At that

moment I felt as if my life was over. See God had given my

mother who was an Angel a second chance at life, and then Satan took that opportunity to deceive her.

My mother fell in love with him and he used her kind heart to give him a child. I am the princess of hell, and he wants you as my prince. That is what he saw in you and now he will stop at nothing to get you back.

You have to finish the test that Satan has set in place for you and if you do this we will be welcomed back with open arms. If you disobey Satan he will track us down, and we will both born in hell for an eternity. I am Satan's child, and he will kill me for not following his orders, and if you don't follow what he says he will destroy you. I love you Michael and I am truly sorry.

What I am about to tell you will change your life forever; he wants you to embrace your evil spirit completely. In order to embrace your evil spirit completely and fully turn your back on God you must do the unthinkable. You must commit an act so horrific that you couldn't even forgive yourself. You must be willing to do whatever it takes to go into the darkness and embrace it. What Satan wants of you is to kill your family. Michael you must go into their home and kill them all. You must look your family in their eyes and kill them without any hesitation. You can't back down from this Michael because if you don't our souls are at stake. I am truly sorry Michael I wished there was another way."

I don't care about what he thinks or what you think. I will not kill my family. I will rather burn in hell, then to kill my family. I have accepted my fate, so now it is your turn to accept yours. I know that God has turned his back on me, but I will not turn my back on my family. I can't believe you did this to me. I thought you loved me and now you are here telling me that I have to kill my family. Satan had forbidden me from coming ~~here~~ back home, ~~so~~ He sent me I could come back ~~and destroy~~ to destroy my family. ~~You are the worst because~~ I fell in love with you and you lied to me.

Everything you told me was a lie and you still say that you love me. Satan should be proud of you because you did break my spirit, but you forgot that my love for my family could never be broken. So, I suggest that you go back to hell because I will not be returning with you. Michelle grabbed my arm, and says, "If you don't do this then they will come for you. I can't lose you Michael. Michael I don't know any other way that we can stop him. Satan is too powerful and God will not intervene. I have been waiting on God to come get me from Hell ever since Satan took me down there.

I never got an answer from God so I gave up. It was easy for me to break the spirits of others because my spirit was already broken. They usually gave into greed, lust, or power after a few months of working with us. You are a strong person Michael, but you can't stand up to Satan alone."

So, everything that happened in that cell was just to set me up, so I can be the prince of hell. You mean to tell me that Satan has been grooming me as the prince of hell. Satan wants me to be your husband, and this is how he wants me to be like him. I don't care, so you tell him to go to hell!

Do you hear me Satan; Go to Hell! I am not going to kill my family, and there is nothing you could possibly do to make me. I will never give into your will Satan. I am my own boss, and because of you I will conquer any obstacles that you put in front of me. SO, IF YOU WANT ME SATAN, THEN COME AND GET ME!

Michelle took her dagger out and said, "If I can't get you to kill your family then he wants me to kill you. I have to take you back to hell die or alive. Satan wants you as his prince or for you to burn in hell for all of his followers to see. I can't burn in hell; I won't be able to take it. I am so sorry but I have no other choice. There is more going on then you know, but we're running out of time!"

I pulled out my dagger. Michelle you love me, but yet you still want to take everyone I love away from me. You are supposed to fight for the one you love, and stand by their side. I would die for you, but you aren't willing to die for me. I would march into hell, and challenge Satan himself to save your soul. I love you more than life itself. I can't do what you ask of me and I can't kill you.

So, here is my dagger Michelle do what you must. I dropped the dagger on the ground. I got on my knees and held my arms out. I closed my eyes, and held my head up to the sky. Tears started falling down my eyes and I started feeling God presence on me. It was pitch black dark and it started to rain. The rain started to wash my tears away. I could feel Michelle picking up the dagger and walking towards me. Michelle put the dagger back in my hand and pulled me up. Michelle started to cry again and said, "Get up they are coming for us. We have to stop them.

They will come in the form of an army and they won't stop until they are able to take us back to hell. They will also try to take your family, so we have to cut them off. I am so sorry for all that I have done, but I promise you that I will fight until the end. I will stand by your side Michael. I love you Michael and I will protect the ones you love because I love you. We don't have much time because when they come they will not stop. They will come with everything they have and we have to come with everything that we got. We are both powerful, but we have to be at our best to stop them."

Michelle we will stop them because we have the love for each other that will conquer all. I see them coming up the street! It looked like a million soldiers charging towards us. We started firing at them with all our energy, and slashing them with our daggers. I knocked down one, and two will come at me and the same with Michelle.

We kept on knocking them down, and more kept on coming. There were hell beasts, soul keepers, demons, and his followers all coming to rip us about. Everything Satan had at his disposable was headed our way. The only thing we could do now is hold our ground, and fight until the end.

Whoever destroyed us and brought us back barely alive would be in Satan good graces. So, they started biting us. The hell beast jumped on top of Michelle and I stabbed it in the neck, and it fell backwards. A demon grabbed me from behind, and started slashing my back with his razor sharp nails. I fell to the ground, and a soldier of hell stabbed me it in my leg. Michelle threw him into a crowd of charging demons. I got up, and kept on fighting. It seemed like the more of them we destroyed the more they kept coming.

Michelle was bleeding from all over and so was I. The fight was taking its toll on us. It was a matter of time when the army that Satan sent to bring us back would overcome us. So, Michelle and I looked at each other knowing what we had to do. Michelle and I held each other hand. We took all the energy we had inside, and threw it at the army. It was everything we had inside of us; it was all the evil that we had buried deep inside.

We let everything go, and we direct the attack to the army. The ball of energy was a direct hit on them all, but the damage was already done. The army was destroyed, but we were only hanging on our lives by a thread. Michelle and I fell to the ground. I crawled over to Michelle, and pulled her body into my arms. Please don't leave me Michelle; I love you so much.

OH GOD PLEASE HEAR MY CALL. I KNOW THAT I HAVE LOST MY WAY. BUT I NEED YOUR HELP TODAY. PLEASE HELP US LORD. I AM SO

SORRY FOR WHAT I HAVE DONE, BUT WE NEED

YOU HELP. PLEASE; OH PLEASE GOD HELP US!

It started raining again, and Michelle started to walk

up as she held onto my hand. She kept on saying I am so

sorry God please forgive me, and not to blame Michael for

what he has done. Michelle hangs on; don't you leave me

Michelle!

GOD I NEED YOU MORE THAN EVER NOW. I

KNOW THAT I DONT DESERVE YOUR MIRACLES,

BUT I DONT KNOW WHAT ELSE TO DO. I DONT

KNOW WHO ELSE TO TURN TO; SO CAN YOU

PLEASE FIND IT IN YOUR HEART TO HELP US?

HELP US PLEASE; OH GOD HELP US!

I started to feel a little dizzy, and my eyes started to

get heavy. Michelle hand that was gripped on mines started

to loosen. As her hand loosened I felt my eyes getting even

heavier. I fell back, and Michelle hand was off of mine. I

could feel our bodies moving, but I didn't know where we

were going. When I awakened I was in a room and it was really bright. I was an all-white room with a white bed that I was sleeping on. I walked out the room, and I saw a shadow of a man walk down the hall. I went behind him, and he was standing near the balcony. I walked towards him, and I could feel a connection with him. The guy turned around and it was my father.

How? Why? I am dreaming? Are you my Dad and why am I in heaven? Where is Michelle? I didn't understand what was happening, and why God brought me to heaven after all I have done. I crossed the line and committed so many sins that I thought that I was so far gone from God's Grace.

My father turned to me and said, "Son do you remember when you were five and you asked me what makes a person a good person. I told you that it is not the good deeds that a person does, but it is the experiences the person goes through that defines who they truly are.

The path you were on was leading in the wrong direction. After I passed away you had to step up as the man of the house. I know that things weren't always great, and we made you move away when you were little. I hope you know now that we were only trying to protect you, and all we ever wanted was the best for you. In order to keep you safe we had to let you go.

You were always there for your mother and your sister. But I could see it in your heart that you felt no one was there for you. I see how hard you worked and how frustrated you were not having a successful job. Not having a soul mate and having to see your family struggle to pay the bills. You felt that you let them down, and you let yourself down. So, I went to God and I asked him to help you. So, God put you on this journey and you had to walk to the road of life to find your way home. You had to go through hell to get to hell."

So, are you telling me this was all a test, or some kind of journey for me to see the light? Dad I had to go through pain and suffering in hell. I almost died fighting for my life. Michelle sacrificed her heart and soul for me. I understand that God had put me on this path and I had to walk down this these roads to find my way to the truth that has set me free. So, everything that happened to me was planned? What would have happened if I never came back to earth? What would have happened if Michelle never stood by my side? Would I have made it here today if I had given up?

My Dad walked over to me and said, "Sometimes we search for answers that we already know, but don't want to accept. We go through life sometimes expecting God to do everything for us. God is always there for us, but we have to be willing to meet him half way. We can't expect God to do everything for us, and we can't understand what is true to us until we see the truth in our lies. We lie to ourselves to hide behind the pain, but it is the pain that makes us stronger.

Son you are a great man, yet you hide behind a wall of fear. You are afraid of succeeding because you think when you do people will see you as a fraud. You think once you succeed you will eventually fail again. You got yourself believing that you aren't good enough to achieve your goals. I am here to tell you as longs as you have faith, and the God in your heart will can do anything you set your mind too. You must believe in yourself because God believes in you."

My Dad turned around and hugged me. My Dad told me that he loved me and we started walking. Heaven is so beautiful and peaceful. Heaven is nothing like hell. Everyone up here is happy, and it feels like home to me. I can't believe I was just in hell yesterday, but now I am in heaven. I get it now, but as I kept on walking I can't help but think where Michelle was. I looked down the next hall, and it's Michelle. Michelle has a white gown on, and she looks so happy to see me. She runs into my open arms. Michelle this is my Dad and Dad this is the love of my life Michelle.

Michelle smiles and said, "I have already met your Dad and he's a great man. I woke up just before you did and you were sleeping so peacefully so I let you sleep for a little bit longer. We talked a little bit about our past encounters. But that will have to wait for another day Michael. I am so sorry it had to come to this, but I am glad that one thing came out of this. The only good thing that came out of this is being able to love you Michael. I love you more than you will ever know."

So, whatever happens here on out I am happy that we got out of hell and I can thank you for that. So, Dad what will happen to us now? Do we stay up here in heaven? Do we go back to earth, or are we getting sent back to hell? I have been gone for so long that I don't know what to expect when I go back. I don't know if we could go back, so much has changed on earth. Michelle and I created so much destruction on earth. I don't know if we even deserve to go back to earth, or even stay up here.

My Dad told us to sit down and said, "Michael you will return back to earth as if nothing happened. You will return back to the day, and time you left to go to Crossroad Park. You will arrive at Crossroad Park at 12 midnight, and be able to go home. Everything will go back to the way it was, and you will be the only one who remembers what had happened. You are now in control of your destiny, and you now know what road you must travel to stay of the righteous path.

Dad I need you to help out a friend of mine. I told my little buddy that I would protect him, and I left him all alone. He is not capable of fending for himself. This guy is very fragile and timid. Please tell me that you can ask God

253

to send someone to protect him! I can't go back without at least trying to do everything I possible could to save him.

My Dad stood up and touched my shoulder and said, "Son I promise you that God is watching over all of his children. Your friend Andrew is on his own path, and he has to walk it alone. You can't always be there for him my son, but what you can do is pray for him. You have to live your own life, and not always worry about things beyond your control. Andrew came to you in a dream didn't he?

How did you know that Dad?

My Dad smiled at me and said, "I am in heaven son it is my job to know these things. What you are feeling is guilt Michael. You aren't able to protect Andrew all the time so it is eating you up inside. Andrew wants you to let him go and live your own life. You have to walk your path, and let him walk his. If you continue trying to be on two paths at once, then you are going to end up on a path of destruction. Live your life Michael and let Andrew live his. Andrew will be find, it is you that I am worry about.

I also see that you have forgotten how good my sister has been to you. Your Aunt Katherine has always been good to you, and only wants the best for you. You have to trust her and believe what she told you were for your own good. Don't challenge her just know that she wants to keep you safe. Remember my sister has always kept you on the right path, it is when you wanted to rebel is when you lost your way. Everything isn't at all what it seems.

My Dad smiled at me and said, "I am in heaven son it is my job to know these things. What you are feeling is guilt Michael. You aren't able to protect Andrew all the time so it is eating you up inside. Andrew wants you to let him go, and live your own life. You have to walk your path, and let him walk his. If you continue trying to be on two paths at once, then you are going to end up on a path of destruction. Live your life Michael and let Andrew live his. Andrew will be find, it is you that I am worry about."

I will try Dad, and thank you for never giving up on me. So, now what will happen to Michelle? Is there anything I can do to help Michelle?

Michelle God has already determined your fate, and I am sorry I can't change it. She will not be going back to earth with you. She has to face the consequences of her actions. God will now judge you Michelle, and it is in front of him that you must ask for his forgiveness and repent. Today is your Judgment Day Michelle, and I hope that you ask God to forgive you for your sins, and that he show mercy on your soul. I have to go my son, but remember this I love you both. I am proud of you both.

Michelle God always loved you and heard you calling out to him. Michelle he never gave up on you and you shouldn't give up on him. I will see you both soon, but it is time for me to go. Tell your mom that I will always be there for her and she will never be alone. Tell her that I hear her and that as long as she holds onto our memories I will always be there in her heart.

Our past meeting hasn't always been the best, but I knew back then that you were destined to do something special. I could see it in your eyes even back then that you were lost. You needed something or someone to show you the way. All you needed was someone to share the love that you had in your heart, and someone to give you love in return. The thing that we are missing in life has always been right in front of us. I am glad that you finally found what you were searching for."

Michelle smiles at my Dad, and says, "I wasn't searching for your son. I am truly happy to be in love with your son. I know that this journey was a test for Michael, but my situation is different. You understand as well as I do that nothing is meant to happen for me, but I am truly thankful to have found love despite of all this."

What are you talking about Michelle? What is going on? Can someone tell me what is happening right now? I thought all the ridicules and questions where all answered. What can possible be so bad that it can break us apart, or make things worse. Whatever dark secrets you have Michelle I will always love you no matter what.

My Dad stands up, and says, "Now is not the time. You have to go back. Your time here is done. The truth will eventually come to the light, but for now you will have to be happy for with what you have. I know that you still have some questions, but you have to realize things will all fall into places when they are meant to. You can't rush fate, but what you can do is believe that God will always make an opportunity for you to receive your blessings. It is time my child. Tell everyone that I love them, and I never stopped loving them. I will continue to watch over you all. Good bye my son I will see you soon."

Why am I so tired? I can't keep my eyes open, but it is time for me to go. My Dad told me everything I wanted to know. Even though Michelle and my Dad past encounters that had brought new questions to the surfaces I was satisfied with the answers I were able to get. I was happy that I fell in love, and was able to go back home. I hope God will let me take my blessing back to earth with me. I can't imagine my life without Michelle in it.

I must stay awake I don't want to wake, and Michelle was just a dream. If this is the only world Michelle exist in then I want to stay here. Please Lord don't take here away from me. As I yelled Michelle got closer and closer to me. My voice started to get lower and lower, and my eyes stated to get heavier and heavier.

Chapter 11

I couldn't hold me eyes open anymore, and my Dad was walking away. I held Michelle in my arms tight. I didn't want to let her go. I didn't know when I returned if she would be there with me. So, I held on tight, and kissed her as we both closed our eyes. I woke up a few minutes later and I was at Crossroad Park. A bus pulled up and it was Paul.

Paul said, "Michael I am glad to see you made it. I never doubted you for a second Michael and I see that Michelle made it as well. You had to see the truth for yourself Michael. I could only take you so far and you had to travel that tough road alone because it is when you are alone is when you need God the most. You were drifting away from us, but you came back. No matter how far you thought you went down the wrong path you should always know that God and your Dad have always been there for you."

Someone tapped me on my shoulder and I turned around it was Spencer. Spencer what are you doing here? Why did you steal my ticket? Don't tell me that you are working for God; are you? I understand now and I don't blame you for anything. If anything I should be thanking you both, because I would have never met Michelle. I would have never realized how much I already had. I realized that I had everything I already needed and the things I wanted weren't as important as I thought it was.

Spencer gives me a hand shake and said, "Michael you have to believe that anything, and everything is possible if you just believe that you can do it. The only way something that is impossible is beaten if you believe that nothing is impossible when you have the love of God in you. You must find the strength to carry own even when you think all hope is lost. You must pick yourself up when you fail. It is when you fail you learning the true value of achievement.

We must first look in ourselves to see who we are, and if we believe in the Lord we will see the truth in his reflection. When you feel the devil breathing over your shoulder turn to God, and he will stand by your side. I am proud of you Michael you made it. The bus stopped and I can see my apartment from here. The bus pulled at the corner of my families' house, so I had to walk the rest of the way. I stopped and starred at the bus as Paul and Spencer waved goodbye.

The bus got a half a block up the street, and disappeared. I finally realized what I was searching for all along was always inside of me. It took this journey to make me realize that I didn't need to go searching for answering, but realizing that within me lies the truth that could had made me avoided all of this chaos that I had to go through. But I am glad that I went on this journey because I found true love in the process.

I walked into the house and my family was waiting for me. My mother hugged me as I walked in, and told me never to scare her like that again. My sister told me that they called my job, and they told me that you had left hours ago. We also been calling your phone and you didn't answer.

My mother slapped me, and said, "Where have you been? I went out with a friend, and we lost track of time. We went out to dinner, and went for a walk afterwards. I am sorry for not calling, and it will never happen again. I promise that for now on I will call, and never let you worry about where I am. This might not make since, but Dad said that he loves the both of you. He also said that he will always be there for you Mom, and never leave your side. Mom, said, Are you ok Michael? I will take your word on that, and for some reason I know that he is. What I want to know now is where the young lady was? Did she drop you off, and go home? And why this is the first time you are mentioning her. What is her name and what is she like?

I didn't know what to say, or think. Everyone was different. It was like it was before I left on my 13th birthday except my Dad wasn't here. My family looked, and treated me like they were all happy to see me. I felt loved, and saw smiles on everyone's faces. This was worth coming back home too. I had my family back, but having Michelle here with me would make it even better.

Mom her name is Michelle and she is beautiful. I am in love with Michelle. It feels like I known her an eternity. She is the type of person that would walk through hell with you, and stand by your side. I love her, and I can't wait for you all to meet her. But you all will have to wait to meet her because she had to go away for a little while. I don't know when she will return.

My sister put her child in his crib, and said, "Why do we have to wait to see her? If you love her so much;

why can't we see her? Is there something you not telling us Michael? Is she married, got kids, or are you ashamed of showing her to us. Do you think that we would embarrass you in front of her? Why can't we see her?"

I didn't know what to say, but then there was a knock on the door. I opened the door, and I couldn't t believe my eyes it was Michelle. I stood there in front of the door looking at Michelle in total shock. My mother pulled her in and said, "Hi I am Michael's Mom, and this is his sister Nicole. And the little bundle of joy in the crib is Jasmine. And you must be Michelle; it is a pleasure to nice to meet you.

He was just talking so highly about you, and I am glad we got a chance to meet you now then later. Michelle turned to me, and said, "I had to pee sweetie, and I can't hold it any longer." Let me show you to the bathroom Michelle, it's this way. I went into the bathroom with her and asked her how this was possible. I thought that God had other plans for you. I thought that I would never see you again. I thought that this was the end of the line, but here you are right in front of me alive.

I am so happy to see you, and so glad it get to live the rest of my life with you. You are here to stay? Please tell me that you are here to stay? I can't lose you again Michelle, so please tell me that you are here to stay?

She started laughing, and said, "Calm down sweetie I am here to stay. God gave me a second chance, and told me to never stop believing in what I can do. He told me to trust in his words, and he will bless me. I didn't believe in his words, but I now believe that no matter what happens I know that he has my back.

I use to come to earth sometimes, and see people suffering. I see hurricanes destroy cities, and the government do nothing. I thought how a God that loves his people can allow bad things to happen, but I realized that it starts with us, and ends with God. It is up to clean up our own mess, and it's what we do in the midst of tragedy that will show who really are Gods people. I didn't believe in love before, or believe that I could be anything other than a failure. I now believe that no matter what obstacles is ahead of me I will believe in myself and overcome them all. I will walk down the road of life with God, my family, you, and all of your love with me. I know now that it's hell on earth.

No matter what road I choose to take in life that I will experience it, but I will become a better person because of it. The sky is the limit for us now and we must cherish each moment because we knows how it felt when it was our last. No longer will I take my life for granted, and I believe that even though humanity is fragile I still want to help make it better."

My mother started knocking on the door and said, "Don't be making any babies in there." We all started laughing. Michelle and I came out of the bathroom and set on the couch. We talked for about an hour and then my

Mom said that she had to get ready for work. Michelle and I said goodbye to my Mom as she drove away in her car.

My sister Tiffany pulled me to the side and says, "It is too late for her to be driving home. Mike you should tell her to stay the night. I don't trust the people out there and it's too late to call a cab. By the time a cab comes she would be exhausted. I don't like strangers spending the night, but its fine if she is a friend of yours. To give yourself peace of mind have her stay because you don't want to sit up and want to see if she made it home."

I told Michelle to stay the night and she did. Michelle slept beside me, and it felt great. Everything was as it should be, and everyone was happy. Even though everything went back to the way it was I felt like I had everything in the world. I had something priceless that money couldn't t buy. I had my family and Michelle the love of my life. I had God and my Dad watching over me. I had everything I needed and I knew someday I would get everything I ever wanted. And if I happen to not get everything I wanted, then I will still be happy.

I was thankful for what I had, and not worried about what I thought I needed. I started to fall asleep, and it was about 1:30 am. My phone started to ring and ring so I answered it. The guy said, "It is not over, and I will get you both in the end. I told Michelle that you both wouldn't be able to escape my wrath. God may have won this battle, but in the end I will win the war. Michelle is my princess and you are my prince. I own the both of you and I will come for you both. You can't hide from me and I will destroy everything you love if you choose not to obey me. Get all the sleep you need Michael, and tell Michelle to get some rest because you both are going to need it. I will see you both real soon."

I look out the window and I see a black Mercedes out in front. Sheriff Judas is standing in front of the car. There is a man looking up at me from inside the car in the back seat. We both looked at one another and he stares

back at me with a smile. I recognize that smile and it sent

chills through my whole body. Michelle walks over to the

window with me and we both stood there shocked.

Michelle grabs my hand and says, "I love you

Michael and no matter what happens from here I will

always love you. You have made me the happiest person

on earth. I can't imagine my life without you. Whatever

my father has in store for us I know with you and the Lord

by my side I can get through anything. Thanks for not

giving up on me and seeing passed who I was."

Michelle puts a smile on my face and as he

continued to look at us I didn't fear him anymore. I was

happy, blessed and felt that I had everything I could

possible want. I don't know why I was so afraid of life and

thought that my life wasn't worth living. Some people

believe that the greatest trick the day ever played was

making us believe that he didn't exit. I however, believe

that the devil's greatest trick was making us believe that we didn't exist.

Sheriff Judas got back in the car and as he drove away Satan waved good-bye. I don't know if Satan was finally able to unleash his reign of terror on earth or not. What I do know is that he made it clear that he wanted us back. Maybe it was our eyes playing tricks on us, or Satan trying to put fear in our hearts.

There is one question that I don't have to answer and that trusts what I do know. I can't say to someone that you have to put your faith in God because not everyone believes in God. We all have our own beliefs, so I believe that we have to have faith in what we believe. So if I want to worship a rock, then I will not let anyone change my mind. I can't expect someone or something to magically give me everything I want. I have to have faith and believe in myself.

We tend to believe that we don't matter and that we are all alone. Just because you aren't recognized by the ones you want to see you don't mean that no one cares. Because when you feel all alone look to the sky and you will have your love one's smiling back at you. The only one that can defeat you is you. So, the devil is coming for me, so with God by my side I welcome that battle. With God by my side I fear no evil.

My mother overheard Michelle and I talking and I started crying. My mother sat in the chair in the kitchen mumbling, "I am so sorry; what have I done?" I walked to my mother and told her that everything is going to be ok. I told her no matter what the problem is we can work it out. I have faith in my family and God. So, my mother raised her head and look into my eyes.

My mother with a bit of hesitation said, "I am the reason Satan has come for you. I know you went to see your father and I know that Satan will not give up until he has you. It is because of me that Satan has your soul. I was young and foolish when I was approached Satan. He promised me that if I gave him my first born son I would live to be a hundred years old.

At that time I was diagnosed with cancer and I had 6 months to live. I did everything I could. The doctors said that there was nothing else I could do. Your father and I were giving up until Satan came to us with an offer. At first we both said no and told him that we have faith in God. I was getting worse and your father was getting worried.

So, I made the deal with the Satan for your soul. We didn't think that we would have any more kids. A few years past and then I gave birth to you. I remember holding you in the hospital and your father was sleeping in the chair by my bedside. I was getting sleepy so I buzzed for the nurse to come get you. I was a little dizzy, but when I raised my head I saw a young woman dressed in white. I was a little dazed from the medicine, but I had a bad feeling that this wasn't a nurse. She only said one thing and that was, "Enjoy the next few days with your son because he now belongs Satan. I will return for him by week's end."

Before I could even focus my eyes on her; she was gone within a blink of an eye. I was so terrified and I just started screaming. Your father woke up in a panic. I told him that they came for our son and for him not to let them take you always from us. Your father was a proud man, so he without saying a word he got up and left.

After he left I was sitting in the hospital room with you in my arms. It was my last day at the hospital and your father was nowhere to be found. I was getting worried and all I could think about was everything is going wrong. It was a moment that your father, your big sister and I were supposed to be enjoying.

I called your Aunt who was watching your big sister and your Dad wasn't there. It was getting close to the time that I was supposed to check out and the nurses where getting my things ready for me to go. Your father comes walking in my room as the nurse gave me the papers to sign to leave. Your father put you in the car sit and kissed me on forehead. Your Dad whispered in my ear, "Don't worried anymore; everything is going to be ok. I fixed everything, so we can be a family."

I was so happy, but I was curious about how your Dad fixed everything. Every time I asked your father what he did to fix thing he avoided the question. After a few months of asking your Dad what he did I gave up. I stopped asking your father and realized that we were happy.

We were so afraid that someone would come after you that we had you live with your father's sister in Louisiana. I didn't want to lose you, but after your father died you wanted to come back home. You had barely turned 18 years old when you came back home and in the back of my mind I was still worried about your safety.

Having you back home felt great, but at the same time I was stressing out. I didn't know if they would come for you because your Dad passed away. Part of me always felt that your Dad went to heaven, so that meant that Satan would send someone to finish what he started. I know I told you that your father died of a heart attack, but I didn't feel like you were ready to know the truth. I felt like you deserve to know now and I think we are running out of time.

So, when you were home we kept our distance from you. We didn't want to get too attached to you, and then you are taken away from us. No one wanted you to feel left out, but you had to see it from our prospective. We felt so bad ignoring you, but when you returned in the back of our minds we knew that it wasn't over. If I had known this would happen, then I would have given up my soul a long

time ago."

Chapter 12

I can't believe you didn't tell me that you knew the whole entire time. I went on this journey, and suffered because of a deal made before I was born. I despised people who gave up their souls for any reason. You should have told me the truth a long time ago. Maybe I could have done something. Maybe I could have helped!

My Mom wipes the tears from her eyes and says, "Two weeks before you turned 18 years old your father was in a car accident and he was badly hurt. I sat in the hospital with your Dad. Your Dad grabbed my hand and told me the truth about how he fixed the problem that has haunted me all these years. Your father made a deal with Satan to take his soul in exchange for him not taking your soul. He told me that the man who hit drove a black Mercedes.

I cried and your Dad looked into my eyes. Your Dad said, "I am so happy to have you and our two kids. I lived a long and amazing life. I couldn't have asked for a better life and now I can die knowing that I did all I can."

Your father closed his eyes and passed away. I was devastated and I felt this strange feeling. I looked out the window and it was a black Mercedes out in front. A man in all black was standing by the car and in the back seat was Satan. He smiled at me and then the man got back in the car.

That was the last time I saw them and today was the day I felt that same strange feeling. I knew when you and Michelle were talking about a black Mercedes out in front and a man standing beside it was Satan. I knew then that Satan went back on his word and would be coming for you.

The agreement was that Satan was supposed to take your Dad's soul; instead your Dad went to Heaven. From that day forward I was treading the day that Satan would take your soul, or send that mysterious woman back to come get you. I don't know what I would do if something ever happened to you. I couldn't live with myself knowing that I was the cause of all this."

I looked at my mom and assured her that everything would be fine as my dad told her. I am 26 years old now and that was 8 years ago. I escaped hell, so he had his chance to get me. I am not afraid of him, or who he will send to come get me. I have my family, Michelle and God on my side.

I do remember one thing though, my mom said. My mom gets up from the kitchen table and says, "The mystery women carried a white dagger with her. I thought with all the medicine I took I was seeing things, but now thinking back she had a dagger with her. I wish I could remember more, but it was so long ago."

At that moment I knew who it was and was in a state of shock. I turned around and looked at Michelle. Michelle and I looked at one another for a moment.

Michelle smiled at me, but this time it felt eerie. Michelle pulled out her white dagger and stood there for a moment.

Michelle said, "You weren't supposed to leave hell. I wasn't supposed to fall in love with you. I was weak and naïve at that time. I assure you that this time around you will not be coming back. I still love you and I always will, but you belong to my father Satan. I should have taken you when I first visited your mom, but my orders were to wait and so I did.

Your Dad made a deal with Satan in exchange you were allowed to live. But Satan doesn't like playing fair, so he sent Sheriff Judas to make sure that your dad's deal was broken. After your father untimely demise the first deal was back and I could get your soul at any time. So, I waited for the right time to get you. I wanted to wait until you were at your best to make me taking you feeling like you were at your worse. I wanted you to fight and plead for your life.

For years it felt like you were giving up and were almost welcoming death. I knew that I had to wait for the right time to get you. When you arrived in hell I knew that you couldn't resist trying to save someone. So, Sheriff Judas set you up and you fell for the bait. It was my job to make you give up on God because you were still holding onto a thread of hope on God's love. My father wanted to strip you of all God's love and show your God even his love doesn't conquer all. No worries Michael you will live like a prince, but you will never be able to return to earth unless it was to take a soul. Beside I can't leave here without the father of my unborn child."

What do you mean unborn child? I should have known something was wrong when you couldn't answer my questions in heaven. Why didn't my father tell me who you were, and what you have done. I would have asked them to send you back to hell if I had known. You will not get away with what you had done. Whatever you have inside of you isn't mine, so take it back where you came from.

Michelle walks towards me, and says, "I have been pregnant for a few months now, but with everything going on I didn't know how to tell you. My plan was to get you back to hell as I was ordered to and then tell you about your child. I guess I was hoping that you would call hell home knowing that you had a child.

Before I could say anything Michelle had her hands around my mother's neck with the dagger pointing at her throat. At this moment I was infuriated and without any hesitation I pulled out my dagger. All the evil that was once inside of me had returned and the power that I thought I left behind overwhelmed me. I felt strong, fearless and wasn't about to back down.

I didn't shed a tear even though I felt like a part of me was dying. Michelle had desperation in her eyes and I knew that this wasn't going to end well. No matter what the outcome was I was going to lose someone close to me. Even though Satan wasn't here with us I know he was somewhere enjoying every single moment. His presence was here and he knew that he was destroying any hope that I thought I had left.

Before I could react my sister started pulling at Michelle, but Michelle was much too strong for her. Michelle threw my sister up against the wall and knocked her unconscious. At that moment I pushed Michelle and my mother hit the floor. I grabbed hold of Michelle and told me Mom to get everyone out of here.

My Mom and my sister grabbed my niece and walked out the door. Michelle pushed me back and smiled. She looks at me and said, "Now that we are alone we can finish this. I am not leaving here without you. We belong together and no one will ever come between us. I had an opportunity to take you when you were first born, but I felt a connection to you. At first I didn't know why, but as years passed I knew that you were destined to be my soul mate.

I felt you when you first arrived to hell, but I knew if I told you the truth you wouldn't want to stay. You still have hope and faith in your heart. I was born in hell and I will never believe in your God. You will eventually come to the conclusion that we belong together and your place in this universe is in hell with me.

We will rule hell right beside my Dad. Everyone will worship us and everyone will fear us. No one will every question you and you will never have to answer to anyone again. Satan doesn't make you believe, have faith, or give you false hope. You believe what you want and do as you please. We take what we want and we don't answer to no one!"

This has to be a nightmare, but I wasn't waking up from this one. Michelle started to cry and I went to console her, but she stuck the dagger in my rib cage. I threw her through the kitchen table and she got up smiling as I got up off the floor. I pulled the dagger out of me and the wound wasn't healing. Blood started to spill out of me like a pipe had burst. I tried to cover the wound with my hand, but it wouldn't stop bleeding. Even though I felt invincible I was bleeding like a human being, and I didn't want to die.

"You will die if you don't come back with me to hell. Earth has made you weak. I love you Michael and I know this life that you are trying to live isn't for you. You can't fight fate Michael. We are meant to be together Michael. You are my prince and father to my unborn child. Come with me Michael and fulfill your destiny."

My destiny is here on earth, I said to Michelle. I will always love you, but I will not be going back with you. If you take my child to hell I will fight for an eternity to get my child back. You can't force me to live the life that you want me to live. Everything that you and your father stand for I oppose. There is nothing you can do that will make me chance my mind.

Michelle tears changed instantly into a smirk and said, "What would you do to get your mother, sister and precious little niece back? My father wasn't here for you; he was here to take your family as an insurance policy. He knew that you wouldn't leave without a fight and even though I am with child you still have the faith in God in you.

If you decide to stay here that is fine with me, but I assure you that your family will not be granted the same luxury that you had when you were there. We will feed them to the hell beasts as snacks. I will make sure to save some scraps to send back to you. Now shall we leave, or do you still need time to talk it over with your Lord and Savior?"

You are really starting to upset me Michelle. I will get my family back and someday my child. I will not give you or your father the satisfaction. You were supposed to be my one true love and my soul mate. Instead you are just as evil as your father. You are heartless and I pity you. You think that this is the life that you deserve to live. You are a sad and pathetic monster.

Call me what you will Michael, but the fact still remains that you have a choice to be made. Free will as your God wants to call it. Either you come with me or save your love ones or you stay here while they burn in hell. I sort of prefer option two; it has been some time since I have seen the souls of the innocent burn in hell. There is nothing better than seeing the soul of the innocent scream for help from their Lord while burning in hell.

Before I could speak my Dad a bright light appear right in front of us. The light was powerful and I felt an immediate connect to it. When the light went a way there stood my father. I was shocked and so was Michelle.

Michelle immediately pulled out her dagger.

My father smiled at me and then looked at Michelle.

My Dad said, "Michelle it's nice to see you again. I was

afraid that this day would come, but together we can win.

There is a lot you don't know, but in time you will come to

realize that nothing is at all as it seems. Your father has

brained washed you Michelle, but I think deep down inside

you know that he always have. Your mother wouldn't

approve of this and she is in heaven as we speak.

I could have told my son everything about you. If I

wanted you to pay for what you did I wouldn't have asked

God to send you back to earth with my son. Your destiny is

here now, and not back in hell. You have been giving a

second chance, and you can't let your father take that away

from you. You have to walk your own path no matter what

the consequences are. This is your choice and your choice

alone.

If you want I can take you to see your mother, but you have to trust me. That man you call your father is pure evil and would destroy the life of even his daughter. He doesn't love you and will sacrifice you to get whatever he wants. You are just a pawn in his game. Don't believe in him you must follower what's in your hurt.

Michelle shakes her head, and says, "I don't believe you and I only trust Satan. My mother was a pathetic human who sold her soul to the devil and burned in hell. Satan gave my Mom everything, but it was her foolish greed that cost her soul. My Mom didn't deserve to live.

My Dad came to earth in search of a bride and met my Mom, but my Mom wanted the power that hell had to offer instead of me. So my Dad burned her for betraying him. My mother tried to take over hell and when she got caught gave up my soul to spare her life, said Michelle.

Michael Sr. stood before me at 6'2 and looks as though he did when he passed away. My father passed away at the age of 50 and I felt that I was robbed the life I desperately deserved. My father was a distinguished man, very confident and a hardworking man. Michael Senior's pride was his amour and sometimes it was his weakness. He is a very wise man and I knew that if anyone could get me out of this mess it would be him. I felt proud to be his son and to stand by my father side to fight this battle. We were not only father and son, but two men fighting for what we believed in.

Son I am sorry I wasn't there for you, but I am here now. I wish I could have done things differently. I wanted to protect you, your mom and your sister. Satan wasn't going to give up on you without a fight so I made a choice. I knew deep down inside that Satan would find a way to double cross me and he did. He sent one of his men to make sure that I didn't live long enough to give him my soul. I thought for sure that I would end up in hell when I passed away, but I ended up in heaven. I knew then that Satan would come back for you.

I had to move fast, so that is why I asked God to bring you on your journey to me. I should have told you everything then, but I wanted you to choose your own path.

My Dad walked towards Michelle and said, "Your mother fell in love with Satan that much is true. It is a lot that your Dad left out. Your mother was forced to live in hell against her will. She didn't want that life for you and she was hoping that your father would give it up. Your Dad promised your mother that he would give up his kingdom for her and her unborn child. I believe that your mom at the time knew deep down inside that he would never change. I think that your mother would be able to tell the story better then I."

Another bright light appeared and when the light went away it was Michelle's mom Gale. Michelle dropped her dagger and went to her knees. Gale walked toward

Michelle and lifted her up by her hand. Michelle stood

there crying as she looked into her mother's eyes. I stood

there looking at my Dad and Gale standing there. It was

like a dream come true even though I didn't know what

was going to happen from here on out.

Gale hugged Michelle and says, "My darling

daughter you have grown since I last seen you. You are a

beautiful woman and I know this must be hard for you.

Your Dad has filled your mind with lies and turned you

against everyone you love. I died trying to protect you, but

Satan and his solider was just too powerful to overcome. It

was a few days after you were born and I overheard your

dad in the next room talking to Judas. He was planning on

taking us back to hell.

Satan can't stay on earth for long without being

unseen and his power is just too great to go unnoticed.

Everyone in the room was all trying to get to Satan to prove

that they deserve to be in his presence. God wanted to

know why he was here and trying to figure out if he was trying to start a war on earth. Evil wanted to either overtake him or join him.

At first your father wanted me to believe that he gave it all up and that he would live out his life as a human. He told me that he was planning on renouncing his thrown and giving up his kingdom for us. No one was more important than us he told me while lying to my face. Your father had a plan and it wasn't giving up his thrown. He wanted a girl that could eventually give birth to the future Anti-Christ. He wanted you to bring him back the heir to his throne and the one that can someday take down heaven.

"You are a liar mother, Michelle yelled out. My Dad wouldn't do such a thing and if he needed anyone to take down heaven it would be me. I am the Anti-Christ. I am the first child of Satan and the rightful heir to his kingdom. Don't think you coming here and your lies will change my mind. My father will have his day and soon

your God will be begging on his knees."

Michael

Dad what is going on? Why are you both here? There was so many questions I wanted to ask, but I felt at the moment every second we wasted we were losing the battle.

I couldn't believe what was going on. What was once a life lesson has turned into a nightmare? But with all that I have been through I knew that this was only the beginning.

How was Satan able to leave hell and come to earth so freely? Satan is the prince of darkness and the emperor of his kingdom. Evil obeys Satan and he can have anyone of his followers to do his bidding. When I collected souls Satan never left his kingdom, but as soon as I return here he is.

There stood my Dad, Michelle with my unborn child and Michelle mother. The power in this room was off the charts. If someone would have told me that that the mother of my child was going to be the Anti-Christ I would have thought they were crazy. By the grace of God if everything works out if I have any more thought provoking question I will just keep them to myself.

My Dad turned to me and said, "We don't have that much time we need to get your mom and sister back. Satan will be watching and setting a trap for whomever comes to save them. He only wants the three of you, but with your help Michelle we can get them back. Satan has to get back to hell because he can't maintain human form for a long period of time and by him being here could start a war with God"

So why don't we start a war and finish off Satan? Satan is free to leave hell from time to time to test the will of God's children. Good and evil are what keep the earth in balance. The devil only does what we allow him to do, but if we keep our faith in God what he does will not matter. You have to understand Satan only power comes from believing that you can beat him only. He pushes you, gives you what you think you want and when you try to fight him he pushes you over the edge. God is always there for you. He creates opportunities to help you make the right choices in life. So a war will not be wise. We have to do this on our own and I assure you that God is with us ever single step we take," my father says with a smile.

By the look on Michelle face I don't think she wants to help or even cares about what they are telling her. I think that Michelle used me to get pregnant to keep me and only believes in what Satan has told her. I put my trust in her and once again I was betrayed by someone who I thought was my true love. From this day forward I will not put my trust in the fresh. I love God and God will put me in position to find my true love.

While I was having a moment of clarity Michelle was gone. She had disappeared and most likely giving her dad the heads up on our plan.

Miss Katherine turns to me and says, "We don't have that much time. My daughter should be telling Satan that we are on our way. Now they are expecting us, so no matter what our goal is to get your family out of there. Michelle has made her choice and if she doesn't want to come back with us then so be it. I love Michelle, but Michelle will have to decide what life she wants to live.

Michael you and Michelle are soul mates. The both of you are destiny to be together. If Michelle doesn't realize what she has with you, then you will have to move on. She will try to use your son, but you will have to stay strong. In time she will see what really matter when she see beyond her father's lies.

During all the chaos I never thought I would be so calm. But I felt that I had to move forward and fight. I knew now that no matter what we go through in life without pain there will never be joy. Nothing ever goes according to plan, but when the chips are down you see who has your back.

The three of us hold hands and teleports ourselves into the mouth of hell. There we stood in Satan kingdom surrounded by his soldiers. In front of us were Satan, Sheriff Judas and Michelle. The soldiers grabbed my Dad and Miss Katherine. My Dad yelled out, "Where is my family. Where are my wife and daughter?"

My mother and sister walked into the room towards Satan. My Dad looked as though he had died for a second time. What was going on? Has my family sold their souls to the devil? My father was speechless and Miss Katherine was crying.

Miss Katherine cries out, "Please just let them go you want me not them. I will do whatever you ask of me, but please leave them out of this. Let them all go and I will spend an eternity by your side."

Satan says, "What makes you think that I am behind this? I admit this was a perfect plan, but I can't take credit for this great moment. See your children wanted to prove that they are worthy of their heir to the throne.

I walked over to my Dad and told him that you were right without pain there would not be any happiness. I will have to go through pain to reach my happiness. I assure you Dad you will be experiencing an unspeakable amount of pain that will bring me an extreme amount of happiness.

My Dad and Miss Katherine cried out why! Michelle said, "My Dad wanted you back and you belong by his side Mom. You think just because you give me some sad story that I will be compiled to fight on your side. I knew that you fought for me and how weak you were. It was easy to manipulate you both."

Dad this all started when you died before Satan could get your soul, so your deal became my burden. If you would have fought for your life, then Satan could have taken your soul. I brought Mom, my sister and niece here to give them the same life that has been given to me. My family will be powerful, feared and live a life of luxury. No one will ever take my family away from me.

"You don't know what you are doing son," my father says. I know exactly what I am doing. I asked to be left alone with Satan, so my family leaves with Michelle after giving me a hug. May I tell the soldier to take my Dad and Katherine to their cell where they will be our prison for an eternity. I wanted a moment alone with Satan.

Satan tells everyone to leave us alone. Satan says, "I didn't think you could do it, but you have proven yourself to me. You have what it takes to help me take down heaven. We will rule the universe and everyone will worship the ground that we walk on.

You will have to do it without Michelle and I. Satan says, "What do you mean?" We knew before we left hell that you were coming for us. Michelle and I had a plan like you said. Our plan wasn't to bring back our parents, but to bring by the innocent people you had trapped down here. As we speak Michelle is releasing the people you imprison and taking them all back to earth.

Satan grabs me by my neck and throws me across the room. Satan says, "They may have escaped, but you will spend an eternity in agonizing pain. You stupid human think you can fool the Emperor of Darkness? There is no way out of hell for you and your friends. By the time they make it to the gate Sheriff Judas will have the beasts rip them to pieces."

Michelle, Katherine and My Dad will handle them. I knew that something was wrong with Daniel and Mary. Amy and I devised a plan just in case one of us made it out of here. She hid the day we made a run for it to Limbo, so she was never captured.

I ran into her a few times when you made me a Soul Keeper. Now she is on how way out with the rest of the people and I was able to keep my promise. No matter what you do to me now doesn't matter. Satan says, "This is my kingdom and you will pay with your soul. I started laughing as he threw me from one side of the room to the next.

I could feel everyone leaving. One by one Michelle, Katherine, My Dad and Amy got the innocent souls out of hell. Maybe this was my destiny and now I feel like I have fulfilled my purpose. Satan can do what he wants with me because I know that God loves me. It took a while for everything to sink in and for me to realize that God never left my side. God has always been there for me and I will always be there for him.

At that very moment I laid there on the floor thinking I started to laugh out loud. Satan says, "Why are you laughing? You will never return to your family and you will burn in hell for eternity." As blood ran from my lips I can feel that I was bleeding internally.

I was in so much pain and I could barely talk. I looked up to Satan with one eye open and said, "I might spend an eternity burning in hell, but as I walk through the valley of the shadow of death I fear no evil. God loves me and he loves you as well Satan.

Satan lifts me up and all the windows open up. Satan moves to the window and the hell beasts are fighting each other as if he was about to throw out a piece of meat. Satan looks down at me and says, "Any last words before my hell beasts devoured you?" I looked up at Satan as if it was the last time I would be seeing him. The Lord is my Savior and he will protect me from harm. Do what you wish. Lord I am ready now. I am ready to come home." Satan lets me go, so now I can finally be at peace and I can go home.

All I can see is a white light surrounding me and I can hear voices in the background. I can't move and I can hear people approaching. What is going on? Am I still stuck in hell? Help me! Can somebody please help me!!! I yelled and I yelled until someone was standing over me. It was two guys dressed in white and they stuck me in my leg with a needle. As my eyes began to focus I saw a woman in a white coat sitting in a chair in front of me.

The lady in the white coat kept calling out my name trying to get my attention, but I felt like a lost little boy. "Andrew can you hear me? Andrew I need you to respond to what I am saying. I need to know if you know where you are and who you are." Andrew can you tell me where you are and tell me your full name?"

Was I dreaming? Could this be happening? I must be dreaming because I can hear Michelle voice. Please let it be Michelle voice that I hear. Everything that I have been through will be worth it if I could spend the rest of my life with her. I don't care what happens to me from here on out as long as I am with her.

Chapter 13

When I looked up I can see it was Michelle sitting there right in front of me. I was so happy, but when I looked down at my arms I was in a strait jacket. What the hell is going on? Why am I in here Michelle? What is going on? I am back on earth, but I felt like whatever was happening wasn't over yet. If this was another test, then I wasn't prepared for it.

Michelle looks at me and says, "Andrew you gave everyone here a big scare. You stopped taking your meds and started to become violent, delusional and calling yourself Michael. You are in a mental institution Andrew you have been here for 13 years now. Do you remember why you are in here Andrew?"

No this can't be I am Michael Savior and Andrew is the name of a kid I grew up with. Michelle what is going on and what are you doing here? Do you work here and why am I in a strait jacket? This can't be happening to me. Michelle what in the hell is going on?

Michelle asked the guys in white to leave the room. Michelle whispers in my ear as she gives me a hug, "Oh Michael I am so sorry for lying to you just now. I had to lie because those two guys that just left the room work for Satan. When we left hell we knew that it would be hard getting you out. Satan wanted to torture you for an eternity. I told him that I wanted to join him and make your life a living hell. The only way I could get next to you without being notice was to pretend as though I was on his side. Please forgive me Michael, but I had no other choice, but to join him to save you.

I have been lost without you Michael. Coming back to hell has been terrifying for me and our baby. Satan has taken his frustration out on me and our baby. I need your help Michael. I need for you to save us and get us all out of hell like you did before. Can I count on you Michael?"

You can count on me Michelle. I knew something wasn't right here. I have to stop Satan once and for all. This wasn't a time for me to think of myself, but for the safety of my family. I saved the innocent souls that were trapped down here now it was up to me again to save the souls of my family. I couldn't save Andrew, but maybe this is my chance to save my family for a similar fate.

Where is Satan now? You have to get me out of this room and then I can handle the rest. I am so happy to see you Michelle. I was starting to give up hope and when you started calling me Andrew I started to believe that I was losing my mind. I don't know what I would do without you Michelle.

Michelle smiles and says, "Don't worry my love everything will be fine when you get rid of Satan. Satan is the only thing standing in our way. The world will be a better place without him in it. You don't want your daughter and me in harm's way? So protect us all Michael from Satan. When your daughter and I are sleeping Satan

comes in our room and plays with us. He calls his games

family time and laughs when we scream from all the pain.

All I can do is sit and watch as he takes our baby innocence

away from me. Our daughter will never be the same

Michael because of her grandfather's sick and twisted

ways. You must put an end to all of this horrific pain that

we have been forced to endure in your absence."

At this moment I am filled with rage and want to

defend the honor of my family. Satan will definitely pay

for what he has done. Michelle releases me from my

straight jacket and tells me there is a knife in the utility

room. So I go to the utility room and grab the knife. I

search the entire building and Satan is nowhere in sight. I

hear the alarm going off. There are people running out of

the building. I stabbed everyone that stood in my way.

All the demons that were coming towards me I had

to eliminate them. I see Satan coming out of an office

probably coming out of a portal from hell. I have to stop him now before he destroys earth. What he did to Michelle and I can't happen to anyone else. I have a family now that I need to protect, and it begins with stopping him.

I pushed Satan back into the office as I stabbed him over and over again. Satan hit the floor and I continued to stab him until his bodied laid their lifeless. Satan didn't have a chance to defend himself and I could tell by his reaction that I caught him off guard. To be the prince of darkness he didn't put of much of a fight. This was way too easy, but the job was done. I had finally rid the universe of Satan. Now it was Satan's turn to burn in hell.

I went to the room I left Michelle, but she wasn't there. I started to get tired, so I laid on the floor waiting for her. I knew she would comeback. She must be hiding from the demons that were after us. Once she find out that I got rid of Satan, then she would come out to celebrate with me. So I lay on the floor waiting for my princess. I kept my sword close to me because I still felt an evil presence around me.

"Put the knife down! Put the knife down and get down on your knees now," A police officer behind me said. I put the knife down and I got down on my knees. I faced the wall thinking that maybe I didn't finish Satan off like I thought. Someone or something had come for me.

Now the Officer told me to stand up, and face her. Was she a soldier of Satan? I wasn't going to let her take my family away from me, or take Satan's soul back to hell. As I sat there I couldn't help but wonder if this was the work of Satan. Did I really kill Satan, or is this more torture that Satan was putting me through.

The Officer told me to turn around. I didn't want to turn around because I was afraid of the truth that was on the other side. When I looked up I couldn't understand why she was sent here, and was this work of Satan. Do you remember me Andrew? She walks over to me and says,

"Do you understand what you have done? I don't have much time Andrew; my backup should be here any minute now. I should have done more to help. I should have been there, but I was too busy wrapped up in my work. Now you have become my work. I can't save you now Andrew.

I never forgave you for killing my sister, nieces, and brother –in-law. Your aunt on your Dad side testified on your behalf, and saved you from a life in prison, but we both know what really happened Andrew. I know that your Dad never raped you, and that you made everything up. I also know that your parents sent you to live with your aunt in Casperton, Louisiana because they feared for their lives.

Before you left to move to Louisiana I came to visit from time to time. Every single time I came to visit I saw the bruises on your Mom, sister, and nieces back. There were cigarette burns on their backs and arms. No one in the house smokes, so I did some searching. I went into your room one day that you were at school. I saw five packs of cigarettes, lighters, pieces of wood with nails sticking out of it, dead frogs, and squirrel heads. I took it to your Dad, and he told me that he would have a talk to you. I also made the rest of your family tell the Dad what was going on, or that I would. When your Dad found out what was going on right up under his nose, he was infuriated.

You were only a child Andrew. You were only a child, but you were so lost. When I found out what was going on in your house it was beyond even my control. I found out this had been going on for years. No one said anything or did anything in fear of losing you. Your Aunt Katherine kept a close eye on you, and made sure everyone kept their mouth shut.

No one wanted to report what had happened, but your Dad came to you with the truth. He told me that you were very upset that he accused you of abusing your family. Your Dad was going to get you some help, and I was going to be the one to take you there. Everyone wanted to celebrate your birthday before you left. I was stuck at work, but I was going to come get you afterwards. When I got off work the house had tape around it, and you were gone. Your Aunt Katherine got to you, and made sure that no one suspected you of any wrong doing.

As Andrew looked at me with a smirk on his face my backup arrived, and put Andrew in handcuffs. I told them to leave us, and I shut the door behind them. I had some unfinished business that I needed to address."

Why I in am handcuff and where is Michelle!

You are in handcuffs because you murdered Dr. Frittermen in cold blood. Michelle is being taken to the police station to be booked and charged for conspiracy to commit murder. She wasn't the mastermind behind all this you were. You got her to do your dirty work so you could kill again.

You knew that Dr. Frittermen had filed for divorce with Michelle. I know when someone is lying to me, and when someone is trying to pull the wool over my eyes. You knew that Michelle thought that you were naïve and gullible, and thought that she could get you to kill her husband. Dr. Frittermen didn't want to give her anything and was going to prove that she was unfaithful throughout their marriage. In their pre-nuptial agreement if proven unfaithful Michelle wasn't entitle to any of Dr. Frittermen's money. Michelle had also taken a life insurance policy out on her husband worth millions of dollars. Since they are still legally married and she was entitled to not only the life insurance policy money, but all his personal assets as well."

This can't be happening to me you are lying! You are working for Satan I know you are. Michelle wouldn't betray me, so where is she really? Wait a minute I know who you are. You are Amy and I helped save you. Why are you doing this to me Amy? Please tell me that you aren't working for Satan now are you?

Amy pushes me to the floor and says, "Andrew I want to help you, but you need to stop lying? I remember when you were just a baby. You were so innocence and filled with so much joy. Now you are a sick and twisted soul that I don't know if the Lord can even save you now.

You didn't want to face what was going on then and you don't want to face what is going on. My old partner arrived at your home, and he told me that you were covered in blood. You were sitting at the table eating birthday cake. It was 1 am in the morning. Your mother and father were in the bed multiple stabs wounds in the stomach and chest wounds between them that killed. You sister and niece were on the kitchen floor with fatal stabs wounds on the back and neck. Your niece was only 2 years old Andrew. You were only 13th years old at that time.

My former partner didn't call for back up, and he didn't call me. I didn't find out what had happened until it was too late for me to do anything. You were already gone, and I didn't know where you were. I had to do some digging to locate your whereabouts.

The first person my partnered called was your Aunt Katherine. He told her everything he saw that day, and then the Chief of my police department, Mayor, governor, and DA swept it all under the rug. I couldn't believe what was happening. Lives were destroyed, but everyone was more concerned with protecting you. Even I started to feel guilty, and started thinking about when my sister, your Mom asked me to look out for you when she dies.

Your neighbors reported hearing calls for help coming from your home and things breaking. When he got there it was too late. Everyone was dead with their heads chopped off and you didn't have a clue to what had just happened. He found a black and a white dagger on the floor in the kitchen by your parent's body. Both of the daggers had your fingerprints on them, it came from the set of Samurai warrior collection your Dad had in the basement closet. There was a trial and everyone in the community was in shock and outraged. The guy that they found was wrongly convicted for the crimes that you committed thanks to some convincing from your Aunt Katherine. Everyone went with her testimony, and since she was friends with everyone evolved with the case it was easy to see what the outcome would be.

Everyone wanted the suspect in custody to be sentenced to life in prison, and was due to your Aunt's lies. You lied to her and told her that you didn't remember what happened. But when I looked into your eyes I knew. I knew that the baby I once knew filled with joy was the definition of pure evil."

My former partner Bobby Clarkson, Katherine, the Mayor, and I all went to high school together. I didn't think that they would all betray me. You killed the people close to me, and all Katherine wanted to do is protect you. I promised them I would keep you safe, but not at their expense. You crossed the line when you murdered your family; my family in cold blood.

I am not Andrew how many times do I have to tell you that. My name is Michael Saviour. I use to live next door to Andrew and I moved from Chicago to Louisiana when I was ten. I didn't come back to Chicago until I was 18 years old. I was very close to my family. My father died when I was about 13 years and my family I are still to this day very close. I would never do anything to harm my family. I love my family. You can call me family right now; they are all at home waiting for me to return.

Amy took her weapon off safety, and said to me, "Listen to me and stop talking. Your file states that you suffer from multiple personality disorder and schizophrenia. Andrew it also says you have a hard time telling what is real and not real. So, I am going to let you in on a little secret Andrew. This weapon that I have pointed at your head is real. And what is about to happen is definitely real. Do you understand what I am saying

Andrew?

I can remember as a child you calling yourself Michael the Savior and saying that he was fearless. Your Aunt said she when you were around her that she didn't think anything of it and thought he was just your imaginary friend. You didn't have any friends in Chicago and you always kept to yourself in school. At times your aunt said that she saw you talking to someone, but there wasn't anyone there.

Your aunt got custody of you, but I tried my best to find out what happened. Your aunt tried her best to keep you away from me. She thought that I would eventually put everything together, and know it was you who killed them all. It was only a matter of time until I put all the pieces to this horrific puzzle together.

You lived with your Aunt in Louisiana and you had fun there as she recalled and you started to find yourself.

You had a lot of friends there, but she could tell at times that something wasn't right. You didn't want to be called Andrew when you were in Louisiana, instead they called you Michael. Since you were a little kid and no harm was being done she went along with it.

Your so called visit home was at your old house where your Aunt had a huge fence around it with chains on it. The only one's was allowed on the premises where armed guards and people she hired to make you feel like you were back at home with your family. I watched her take you in, and before she closed the blinds I saw you talking to someone that wasn't there.

A few weeks later I confronted your Aunt Katherine, and she wasn't surprised to see me. She told me to let it go, and to let you live your life. Everything that happened wasn't entirely your fault. Everything that happened was now in the past, and I should keep it there. I looked at her and said, "Go to hell Miss Katherine, and while you there take Andrew with you.

Your Aunt passed away two years ago from Breast Cancer. Before she passed away she came to see you whenever she could take time off from her busy schedule. During her vacation from work every year since you been here she has spent two weeks at your old home. She made it feel like home for you because you use to get upset when you were off your meds. She wanted you to feel like nothing changed, so you could stay happy. When you got mad you got abusive and bad things would happen.

Your Aunt Katherine loved you and treated you like a son. So I don't understand why you wanted to destroy the lives of everyone close to you. Your aunt and I went to high school together in Louisiana. Katherine was a good woman and like the rest of your family she loved you. Every time I came to see you I wanted to put a bullet in your skull, but I thought about the little baby that I held. I thought about the times I made you laugh, and the smile you brought to my face as a young child. When I started to distance myself from my sister and her kids I noticed that you had changed. I should have noticed it as a police officer it's my job to read the sign.

Your aunt kept you close to her, but when you came back on your 18th birthday alone I knew I had you. You had kept their heads frozen in the basement in the freezer. I guess your aunt, or my former partner never checked the basement. Everyone was too busy trying to cover it up.

So, when you came back home for your 18th birthday, and was sitting at the table eating cake with the heads of your father, mom, sister, and niece it made me sick. I called for backup, so you couldn't get away this time. I had been coming past your house for years waiting for you to return, and waiting for you to make a mistake.

Amy held her gun up to my head as she slammed me against the door and says, "Your Aunt found a way to save you again this time at your trial. She reported at the trial that your Dad sexually abused you as a child. Your Aunt went to the trial with a black eye and bruises on her arm. She told the police that you had saved her from a guy that was trying to rob her, and if it wasn't for you that she wouldn't be alive today. Your Dad never touched your mom, sister, niece, or you. I know this had to hurt you that no one did anything to stop him. Year after year of this going on had to destroy you inside and the anger grew didn't it Andrew?

No one else knew what was wrong with you until you went to trial and a psychiatrist examined you and ran some test. You had them all fooled. After both the prosecutions and the defense's doctors both examined you they both concluded that you were not in the right frame of mind and there for legally insane. They believed that you weren't in control of your own emotions and that the trauma that you had experience as the result of what your father put you through was the result of you losing control on your 13th birthday.

The guy wrongly accused of killing your family committed suicide in jail. There was a rap cheat on him committing murders all across America. No one blinked or shed a tear when they found out he had took his own life. No one blamed your Aunt for wrongly accusing him, or even questioned her motives. Your Aunt Katherine had so much influence that they thought she had done a public service for the community.

Michelle lied to you Andrew and she never loved you. But you knew that she didn't love you, but you had to kill again. You have been a patient here since you were 18 years old. It was either life in prison or life in a mental institution. Michelle as she was being carried out in handcuffs that she was afraid for her life, and that you threaten to kill her if she didn't go along with your plan.

However, we told her that the videotape shows her letting you out of your straight jacket before you murdered her husband. We also told her that we have the murder weapon, and were going to dust it for fingerprints. She confessed to masterminding the murders before she reached the police station. As we speak she is being booked, and will be awaiting trial.

I promise you that you are not going to get away with this. She told us that she stop giving you your meds after she read your chart, and found out who you were. She knew that you were easily manipulated and that if she could get you to embrace your Michael Savior side that you would try to come to her aid.

I am not sure why Michelle confessed when we didn't have any concrete evidence, but I guess we all have to live with the demons that we have inside. All we had on her was being in the building. There wasn't a videotape, and we haven't gotten the results back from the knife yet.

She could have conned her way out of this, and stuck with her fear story. Everyone has the ability to be good and evil. We have free will for a reason, but some of us chose not to take side. You have to be one or the other, and you can't have it both ways. So, Michelle will have to live with what she has done, and so will you.

Off your meds she told us that you thought you were Michael the Savior. You were the champion of the universe. In your chart you kept on saying that you need to save the world from Satan and help rescue your princess. You told the doctors here that you were trapped in hell. Michelle read your file and switched shifts with the other nurse to befriend you. Once Michelle got inside your head you were doing what she told you to do and believed whatever she said.

She took what you had in your chart and used it to her advantage. I am so sorry Andrew for abandoning you so long ago, but the path you have taken ends now. You are

Andrew Earnest Smith III, and my nephew who I love very much. The Crossroad Park Mental Institution in Chicago has been your home for a very long time, but now it is time for you to be at peace.

You could have had a great life, and lived comfortably. Your Aunt Katherine left you everything she had. Your aunt's money, cars, estate, and belongs all went to you in her will. It is still sitting there in your name until you were seen as fit to receive it. I think Michelle knew that, and was going to get you to give it all to her after you both left here. She had a letter signed by her husband saying that you were fit to leave her, and able to be a productive member of society again. Michelle would have had her husband's money and all of yours. She probably was planning on killing you after she had access to your money."

Amy continued to talk about what was going on. I sat there thinking to myself, and started to realize maybe this was the end of the road for me. Everything I have ever

known was a lie to me. I have been tricked, abused and

betrayed. The person I thought I needed to protect was me

all along. How could I have been so stupid? Why couldn't

I have stopped him from touching me and why didn't my

family do anything to stop him.

So, here I sat in the chair a weak, beaten and lost

soul. I searched for answers to why my life was the way it

was and to find my purpose in life. I guess I have my

answers now. Now I know that Andrew and Michael are

one in the same. The paths for both are the same and the

end result is a life in a mental institution. Andrew and

Michael are together at last and no one will ever come

between us again.

So, Michelle isn't pregnant with my child?

"Andrew Michelle isn't pregnant and the both of

you never had sex. Stop it! Stop it Andrew! I don't believe

for a second you don't know who you are? If you don't

stop pretending that you are lost, and confused I promise you that it would be the last thing you do on this earth. Is there anything you would like to say to me Andrew before you go?"

Do you remember Stacy and Donald? Their bodies were found in the janitor's closet at the warehouse. They both were stabbed to death. Mr. Stevenson your former CEO of Whacky Warehouse was the only suspect because his semen was found on Donald's body. Until this day he has claimed that he was innocent, and that they were lovers. The court put him there around the time of death.

But he didn't do it did he Andrew? You were also there, and you saw your chance to kill again. Were they your first targets? Were they the first humans that you killed? No one suspected you, and no one thought about questioning the mentally challenged kid. You had everyone fooled, but me. I didn't do anything out of respect for your parents. I knew if I turned you in, then your parents would be devastated. I kept my mouth shut, and kept my assumptions to myself. There was no weapon, or finger prints to link you to the murders.

Mr. Stevenson and I had a brief discussion as I was taking him into the station on the night of the murder. It was just him and I in my squad car. I asked him if there was anyone else in the building that night other than him. Was there anyone knew about the love affair, and had motive to do it? Your former CEO had his head down, and said, "I shouldn't have got him involved. He wasn't ready, and he was too young to understand. It's my entire fault. I am to blame for all of this!"

He started crying, and said he loved them both. He shouted out, "I couldn't choose between them both. Stacy was at the wrong place at the wrong time. She knew too much, and didn't want to let it go. I told him that I would handle it, but he wouldn't listen. He had to try to fix everything. He wanted to save the day, but I had everything under control.

Mr. Stevenson continued to slip his guts to me. He started to bang his hand against the door of my car. I shouted out, "I should have known Donald was up to something, but I thought I could get away with it. I had it all money, cars, women, and the men of my choosing. I later found out that Stacy followed him one night to my hotel. I had Donald and my little buddy in the car with me. We went into the hotel room like we had been doing for months.

Donald had left his room key at the front lobby for her. Donald and Stacy wanted to set me up and blackmail me. We were in the bedroom having a threesome. I went to the bathroom to freshen up, my little buddy went to go get ice, and when I returned Donald had made us drinks. I started to feel dizzy and disoriented. About a half an hour later I didn't know what was going on. The next day when I came into work Stacy came into my office with pictures in an envelope. She said that she would ruin me if I didn't give her money.

He came in the room a few minutes later smiling and demanding that, they both get large amounts of money in duffle bags by the end of the week. They said that they will ruin me, and will say that I took advantage of a mentally challenged kid. I told them to keep quiet, and I would handle it. As you can see he didn't listen. But this all started with me, and it ends with me.

The pervert paid for what he did. He was only seventeen years old. He didn't know any better at the time, and for us to take advantage of Andrew was wrong. For that I am so sorry, and I wish I had realized that back then. I would have never let it happen."

Mr. Stevenson kept trying to convince himself that he was sorry for what he had done. No matter what he felt, or tried to make amends for the damage was already done.

He was heading to jail, and probably spends the remaining of his life there. I think at this point all he cared about was repenting for his sins. I am not sure what his judgment day was going was going to entail, but if I was him I would have brought some sun block.

No matter where you went Andrew trouble followed you. I wasn't there to protect you. It was as if you were prey and predators could smell you a mile away. I threw you to the wolves like a piece of meat. I abandoned you when you needed me the most.

I would have stopped all this before it started. I felt everything changed when your aunt sent you back home thinking she was protecting you, but it wasn't the solution. Once you got back home it was just the beginning of the horrific events to come.

The interns that previously work here came up missing a few years ago. Do you remember Daniel and Mary? They both were assigned your case before Michelle.

They were good to you, but you couldn't stand to see them too together. Mary brought you books about Saints, demons, and angels. Daniel use to talk to you about his days as a cop, and in the military. But one day I came to visit you they were fighting.

Daniel was reassigned because you had bruises on you, and you told his supervisor that he was touching you. You told me that he was hitting you, and he wanted you to do inappropriate things with him. Mary was engaged to marry Daniel. I was invited to their wedding. A couple weeks before their wedding they both vanished. On several occasion the ordeals found you walking in the woods. You had escaped several times, and each time there were reports of people turning up dead. Your aunt was a very powerful, influential and respected woman. People kept their mouths shut, head down, and you safe.

Their bodies were never found Andrew, but her engagement ring is on the chain around your neck. I didn't

336

notice it before, but I always thought that you had

something to do with it. You have a box of jewelry that

doesn't belong to you in your room. I saw a necklace with a

heart charm that resembles the one in the picture of the

missing girl from your old job. You are wearing a tinker

bell bracelet around your wrist. Your room is filled with

things of missing people that you have had encounters with

over the years. Miss Katherine isn't here to save you now.

Your other aunt didn't want me to go to my boss

with my accusations in fear of putting you away for the rest

of your life. The only reason you aren't in jail is because of

my promise to your aunt Katherine and your Mom. I

promised my sister that I would watch after you and make

sure that you were safe. Now it is up to me to make sure

that you can't bring harm to anyone else."

I knew it was you Andrew that was involved in the

murders of the victims in Louisiana years ago. Even though

your former boss Mr. Stevenson never gave me a name of

his little buddy I knew it was you. You use to say you were expecting your little buddy to show up in here years ago. I knew that it was just a matter of time before you did it again. I didn't think that you would kill your family. The only family that I had left.

When my sister first came to me I should have taken you then, or had you go live with your Aunt Katherine sooner. I thought that you being at home would make you realize how great you had it. Your family was afraid of you, and wanted me to get you some help. At the time I was too busy to care. When I was able to help it was too late. You destroyed the only good thing in my life, and the only thing I could do is wait for you to return. This is entirely fault. I could have; I should have ended it before it all started. This is my problem, so it is up to me to put an end to it.

Since you think that you are in hell, then I will send you back. I don't know what is on the other side, but you will be judged by God when you get there. I am going to send him to you a little bit earlier than expected. Before I go Andrew I wanted you to know that this is all your fault and Michelle will also pay for her role in this as well. Your mom, sister and niece are in a better place now. Your family didn't deserve what you done to them, and I promised them back then I would take care of this. I plan on keeping my promise."

I closed my eyes, but when I opened them back up Andrew was standing behind Amy. Andrew what are you doing here? Please tell Amy that you and I am not the same person. She believes that she is my Aunt, and that I killed my family. Andrew I hope that you didn't kill your family. Did you kill your family?

Andrew looks and me and says, "You are the cause of all this. You let this happened. You could have pretended all of this. Why did you let him hurt me? You let them all hurt me, so they all had to pay. You did nothing to stop them. So, now you will suffer a terrible faith. I warned you to stop what you were doing before it was too late. You didn't want to listen to me, so now you will pay."

Andrew vanishes like a ghost. No Andrew, please forgive me! I am so sorry for leaving you behind. I had to live my own life. I didn't want to go, but I had to find my own way. Please understand that I had no choice. You must believe me my little buddy I thought about you every day and night. See Amy; Andrew and I are not the same person. He is right there behind you. Don't you see him standing behind you?

Amy raises her weapon and says, "Who are you talking to? I don't believe you for a second Andrew. At this point I don't even care if you hear voices, see dead people, or possessed by demons. There is no one behind me. We are the only two people in the room Andrew. If your father did touch you, then he will also burn in hell. No matter what the cause is for you becoming what you are, it must end here.

You have become a very sick and twisted individual, and you know what you did was wrong. If your Dad was to blame for what you become, then he alone should have paid the price. You shouldn't have killed my sister and nieces. I am not going to let you get away with this again. Only one of us will leave this room alive. Your journey will end here, and if you burn in hell for it so be it. If you get there before I do save me a seat.

Andrew reappears behind me, and says, "She is lying to you Michael. She is working for him. She is one of the Keepers of Soul's. She has sold her soul, and now she has come back for yours. You can't let her take you back to hell. This is a trick old friend. Michelle gave you that ring as a symbol of your love that you two shared. Everything you have you have earned as a Keep of Souls, so now she is here to take it all from you. Satan has me trapped in hell.

We all are trapped down here. You have to save us. Michelle and your unborn child need you. We all need you to come save us Michael!"

Just like that Andrew vanishes again, and I don't think he's coming back until I save him. You are a liar Amy, and you are working for Satan. I can see it in your eyes. You tell your master that I am not going back as his soldier, and you will never defeat me. You will have to kill me, and even then I will fight my way out. I will find Michelle, and save everyone. We will escape Satan's wrath once again. Even if it takes the rest of eternity I will not rest until you all pay for trying to ruin our happiness. I know what is real, and I will save the world from Satan once again. I fell in love, I am going to be a father, and I have a family that loves me.

I saved your life and this is how you repay me? I should have left you to rot in the fiery pits of hell. This is just another trick of Satan to take control over me. Satan will never take my soul, and I will send you back to him.

Nothing you can do, or say will make me change my mind.

I am Michael Savior!

I didn't kill anyone. I took souls when I was

working for Satan. I have been to hell and back. What I

have seen and done no one in this world could ever

imagine. I don't know what Satan has promised you, but

you will not defeat me. I will go back to hell, and rescue

Michelle. So you will have to shoot me. Do what you must

because I am getting out of here. With every ounce of

strength I had I rushed for the demon that took over Amy's

body.

Amy pulls the trigger, and all I see is a white light.

As I am falling back I hear the door fly open, and I hit the

floor. I hear a voice in the background. I close my eyes and

the person seems to be moving closer and closer. I feel

another presence in the room, but I don't turn around. I can

feel someone breathing over me, but I can't open my eyes.

The voice says, "I told you that you will burn in hell and

burn in hell you shall."

Made in the USA
Middletown, DE
23 January 2017